FROM

SAUDI

ARABIA

WITH

LOVE

TEEJAY   LECAPOIS

Requiem For A Saudi Woman's Dream

All good things come to an end, and for the bad things, fortunately, it's pretty much the same deal, I guess.

Though my life will end soon, I absolutely refuse to bow down to the forces of adversity which have besieged me for so long.

"Noor Alzahrani, you have been found guilty of murder, for this the sentence is death by swift decapitation, to be carried out in thirty days, may The Most High have mercy on your soul," said the Cleric, Ahmad Ibn Youssef, speaking for the High Court of the Kingdom of Saudi Arabia.

After a sham of a trial, the inevitable verdict was finally rendered, and all of the self-righteous pricks working for the Saudi Judiciary looked at me as though I were a cockroach or something.

I looked at them with my head held high, from the pew of the accused. *What a bunch of smug idiots*, I thought grimly.

A bunch of robed men looking down on a hapless woman from their perches, acting like they're all frigging demigods or something.

Even in the City of Riyadh's Criminal Courts, segregation by sex is very much in effect and quite strictly enforced.

Such is life, and death, in my homeland of Saudi Arabia. There's absolutely nothing I can do about it.

4

I don't know why I thought things would have changed after those years I spent living in Ontario, Canada.

"So be it, as far as I'm concerned, that bastard Ibrahim deserved his fate," I replied without fear or shame, much to the Saudi Judiciary's shock.

A murmur went up among the clerics, and I smiled smugly while glaring at them without flinching one bit.

I'm a condemned woman in a room full of men, I guess I'm expected to be contrite, but all I feel is contempt for the Judicial body before me.

In a socio-political system that treats women as little more than chattel, if more women took blades to their brutish captors, much-needed social change might occur...

5

Other than that, I don't think change along gender lines will ever come to the patriarchal realm of Saudi Arabia.

I felt zero guilt for having murdered my sadistic brute of a husband, Ibrahim Al-Shehri, son of a prominent Wahabi preacher, in his sleep.

All he did was brutalize me, in order to cure me of my Western ways and defiant mindset. As far as I'm concerned, Ibrahim Al-Shehri got off lightly.

I wish I could have made the bastard suffer more. I know I wasn't the first woman he brutalized. I'm glad to have been the last. Too bad he can only die once.

Apparently, my time spent studying Business Administration at Carleton University in the City of Ottawa, Capital of Canada, changed me as a young woman.

As a woman with a mind of her own, I've become a handful. Much more than the average Saudi Arabian Muslim man cares to put up with.

I became the one thing that the Kingdom of Saudi Arabia fears more than its neighbors and geopolitical rivals, Iran and Qatar.

A woman who thinks for herself and rejects the adamantine bonds of tradition, that's the greatest threat to Saudi Arabia's existence...

I'm only five-foot-five, and weigh a hundred and seventeen pounds soaking wet. At my old school in the City of Ottawa, my friends nicknamed me the Saudi Pixie.

While attending Carleton University, I was quite involved with the Muslim Scholars Association, where I rose to the rank of vice president.

I've been told many times that although I'm a small woman, I have a booming voice. Like a female version of Samuel L. Jackson or something.

I used that same loud, fearless voice to address the Clerics, and they exchanged looks of consternation at my defiance.

"You can sit in Judgement of me all you want, I die a free woman," I said defiantly, and I swear I saw them flinch.

"Get her out of here," said the lead Cleric, a sullen-looking, brown-skinned and silver-haired Saudi man with a *Santa*-style beard.

I was led away in fetters by uniformed women working for the Saudi Judiciary, and taken to my cell.

From there I was to be transported to Al Nisa Quarters, the women's wing of the Ulaysha Prison, in the City of Riyadh.

From there, I would remain in my cell until the fateful day of my execution, where I would be beheaded before a gathering of court clerics, soldiers, as well as ordinary men and women.

Deera Square, located in the heart of metropolitan Riyadh, is a location feared by inmates across the breadth of the Kingdom.

It's where public executions occur. Legend has it that a Saudi princess was executed here, but that's before my time.

I am resigned to my fate. For defiant women like myself have to be made examples of. Can't have rebellious women upsetting the order of things, can we?

As I was brought to my cell, I sat down at a corner of the cool, cramped room. My acute claustrophobia crept up on me, just like I knew it would.

In many ways it reminded me of my one-bedroom spot on Bronson Avenue, not far from the Carleton University campus in the City of Ottawa, Ontario.

I remember those heady, wonderful days with great fondness. Indeed, they were the happiest days of my life, now that I think about it.

Not for the first time I lamented the fact that I gave in to the whims of tradition and returned to my homeland, the Kingdom of Saudi Arabia.

Where would I be if I had followed my heart and chosen love instead of tradition ? Not here, certainly.

I'd be far away from this prison, probably in the arms of my beloved Omar. The man whose handsome face and soulful eyes still haunt my dreams...

"Omar," I murmured, and a sad smile came to my face as I thought of my lost angel, the only man I've ever truly loved.

I first met the big and tall, handsome young Black Canadian man while working on a project in the Carleton University library.

He was working on an accounting paper and asked me if I could help. I'm really good with numbers and Omar had seen me work on similar papers as he walked by a few times.

I looked at this handsome young man with the dopey smile, and wondered what he wanted from me...

"Sorry to bother you, ma'am, these accounting problems are kicking my butt, you seem to know this stuff, perhaps you can help me ?" Omar asked, and I looked at him, smiled and nodded.

Seated at my computer, I was on the Canadian immigration website, trying to renew my study permit since the international student office at Carleton University had sent me a warning that it was about to expire.

I was quite busy with important things, and then this smiling, pretty-faced weirdo came sauntering along...

Normally, I am quite reserved around males, and it's not just because I'm a shy person but because of the social and cultural norms of the Kingdom of Saudi Arabia, where I was born and raised.

Young men in my homeland don't casually approach young women they don't know to ask for help with mundane things.

It's simply not done...and there are grave consequences for both sexes when they commit transgressions.

The Mutaween, the religious police of Saudi Arabia, are utterly merciless. Please trust me on that one. They're definitely not to be trifled with.

The Mutaween go about public places in the Kingdom of Saudi Arabia, investigating allegations of misconduct.

Whenever you hear about a gay or lesbian person being publicly executed simply for engaging in queer activity in the Kingdom of Saudi Arabia, unless they got ratted out by friends or family, they were probably found out by the Mutaween.

Oh, and they're even harsher and more unforgiving when dealing with unmarried men and women who engage in, ahem, sexual congress.

As I said before, the Kingdom of Saudi Arabia has executed a princess for adultery back in the day. They're that serious about their morality codes.

Living in the City of Ottawa, Ontario, I experienced quite a cultural shock. The difference between the Kingdom of Saudi Arabia and Canada was like night and day, I swear.

I saw young women walking about in tank tops and short skirts, kissing males and females with wild abandon on the bus, the train or at the mall.

I saw gay men walk about in grocery stores with their adopted offspring. Yeah, it took some getting used to. Patiently I smiled at Omar, and finally answered him.

"Salaam, sure, brother, I'll help you, what is your name?" I asked, and Omar smiled and introduced himself.

When the smiling young man held out his hand, I hesitated and then shook it. Again, I was breaking the rules of my faith and culture by touching an unrelated male, but, hell, whatever, right?

I guess living in the City of Ottawa, Ontario, was beginning to affect me. Damn the Westerners and their strange, at times weirdly wonderful ways, eh?

"Good to meet you, Noor, you're a life saver," Omar said to me, after I basically did his *Introduction To Accounting 101* homework for him.

After Omar submitted the assignment to his prof via email, he logged onto his Facebook profile and asked me if I had one.

15

I smiled and nodded, and he fired up a friend request. Whatever, I thought, for I seldom went on my *Facebook* account.

I wished Omar a good day, then got up to get back to my seat. I've done my good deed for the day.

Returning to the Canadian immigration website, I resumed what I was doing. Renewing my study permit is of the utmost importance.

The Canadian government is really hard on foreign students, especially the ones hailing from Muslim nations.

Canadians act as tough America is the racist and Islamophobic nation, but they're the same way, only more covert about it.

I finished paying for the online transaction with my MBNA MasterCard and then I sipped on some water.

16

I was about to go to the prayer room when I sensed a presence behind me, and abruptly turned around. There he was, Omar, standing about a meter from me.

The concept of personal space seems to be completely alien to Omar, and I am running out of patience.

"Hello, brother, what can I do for you?" I asked politely, with barely concealed annoyance. Omar looked at me and smiled, and then he stepped closer.

A habit of his that I did not like one bit. In the Kingdom of Saudi Arabia, where slavery was legal until 1962, people of African descent use a certain deference in their dealings with Arabs.

It's simply the way of things over there, I'm afraid. I got so used to it that I never noticed it, until I experienced its absence in North America.

As I said before, I was used to dealing with Africans with such a deferential mindset. Omar, evidently, was of a different breed.

In North America, you will see Black men and Black women who are strong, confident and outgoing, utterly fearless no matter who or what they face.

To me, this was a surprising and at times disturbing discovery. It's just the way I thought back then.

Although polite and seemingly friendly, the big and tall young Black Canadian carried himself with a confidence that, to me, seemed strange.

Still, I had a lot to learn. Anxiously I awaited Omar's answer. As far as I was concerned, I'd done the polite and friendly thing and helped him.

What did this fool want and why was he standing so damn close ? My smile froze, and I wasn't sure what to do.

"I wanted to thank you, Noor Alzahrani, say, I was going for coffee, do you need anything ?" Omar asked, and I hesitated, and bit my lip.

Truth be told, I was flat broke. As an international student from Saudi Arabia residing in the City of Ottawa, I receive a monthly stipend of two thousand dollars.

Courtesy of the Saudi government. From this, I must pay rent, which is five hundred dollars, plus groceries.

I receive a U-Pass from the school, which helps for taking buses and trains around Ottawa. OC Transpo sucks but hey, that's life in the City of Ottawa.

I cannot work in Canada according to archaic rules from both governments, so life sucks. After shelling out a lot of dough to expedite my study permit renewal, I was flat broke.

The month would end in three days and then I would have another two grand via direct deposit on my BMO student checking account from the Saudi government.

Until then, however, I was flat broke. Seriously, I only had the food in my tiny fridge at home, that's it. It would seem that circumstances forced my hand...

"Sure, why not ?" I heard myself say to Omar, who smiled. We left the campus library together and

20

headed to Tim Horton's, where Omar bought a coffee, and got me an iced tea and a buttered bagel.

As we sat down, we talked and got to know each other better. Omar Augustin was born in the City of Montreal, Quebec, to Haitian immigrant parents.

Omar was studying Business Management at the Sprott School of Business at Carleton University and intended to become a corporate big-shot someday. I actually found Omar Augustin quite interesting...

"How about you, Noor, what's your dream ? What is your destiny ?" Omar asked me, as he sat across from me at Tim Horton's.

I looked at this tall, handsome and fearless young Black man who wore an Obama T-shirt and blue jeans, and looked into his eyes.

For some reason, my heart skipped a beat and I felt nervous. Omar was something else, I think I knew this even during our first meeting. This brother was not like the others...

"I want to get my degree and return to Saudi Arabia, and start a family," I replied, like the dutiful and pious, obedient young Saudi Arabian Muslim woman whom I was in those halcyon days.

Omar grinned and stroked his goateed chin, and I smiled at him. What's going on inside that young man's head ? A gal had to wonder.

Omar looked at me and licked his lips, almost as if he had something to say, and wasn't quite sure how to say it...

"Noor, that's fine, if that's what you really want," Omar said mysteriously, and then he fixed those eyes on me.

22

There was something almost hypnotically beautiful in those deep brown eyes. A frisson coursed through me, and I paused thoughtfully.

Although I hadn't realized it at the time, Omar was far from the naïve ingénue he first seemed to be. Indeed, there was much more to this intriguing stranger than meets the gaze...

"Of course that's what I want," I snapped, and Omar smiled and held his hands up in mock surrender.

I was kind of pissed by his oh-so cool words and what he was implying. In those days, I got hot under the collar whenever a Westerner brought up things like women's rights in Saudi Arabia.

Seriously, I didn't want to discuss the gender based segregation laws, the fact that women weren't allowed to drive over there, or any of the hot-button topics that Westerners always bring up...

"Easy, Noor, I didn't mean to offend you, I just sense a kindred spirit in you, you see, I like studying business, for example, but my parents wanted me to become a doctor, sometimes, people who love us think they know best, but we must make our own choices," Omar said quietly, and I sighed and nodded thoughtfully.

I could tell that he was sincere. There was something very intriguing about this handsome, sharp-minded and affable young man, and it was making me really uncomfortable...

"Trust me, Omar, I have a mind of my own," I replied, and then, as the young man looked on, I got up, thanked him for the coffee and walked away.

As I made my way to the elevators, I could feel Omar's eyes on me. I turned around, briefly, and he smiled and waved at me with that infuriating grin as though we were old friends.

You've got some nerve, I thought, both amused and pissed off by him. I shook my head and pressed the elevator button, even as a smile crept on my face.

Thus I met the young man destined to change my life forever. When I returned to the library, I saw that I had another friend request on Facebook, and (reluctantly) added Omar Augustin as a friend.

I resume browsing YouTube, watching a video of famous Muslim preacher and author Dr. Zakir Naik, whose work I admire a great deal.

Imagine my surprise when I got another message from Omar, this time on Facebook. Is the brother stalking me ?

"Miss Noor, you are a very beautiful and intelligent lady, I wish to apologize for offending you, I am sorry if my Western ways offend you, I know very little of your beautiful Islamic faith, and would like to learn more, if that's okay with you," Omar wrote.

Pausing thoughtfully, I looked at Omar's message and shook my head. What is it with this strange young man ?

"Salaam, Omar, nothing to apologize, if you are serious about learning about Islam, I'll be happy to answer any question you have," I replied, hoping that this was end to it.

I resumed watching the video of Dr. Zakir Naik. Along with African American Muslim celebrity Dr. Bilal Phillips, he's one of my favorite preachers.

Men whose humanitarian work on behalf of the Muslim community makes us look good in front of the Western world.

"Shukran, thank you sister, by the way, I just learned that my name, Omar, is actually an Arabic name ? How cool is that ? You can reach me by Facebook Messenger online, or on my phone," Omar replied, and then he fell silent for several minutes.

I was about to log off when I received yet another message from him, this one containing a video with thousands of hits on YouTube.

Something about a former Rapper and Hollywood heavyweight whose life changed after he embraced

Islam. An expose on the famous Ice Cube, one of my favorite actors...

"Masha'Allah, you like Ice Cube too ? We're definitely going to get along, my friend," I replied, and then, filled with a strange, weirdly wonderful enthusiasm, I punched Omar Augustin's number into my phone.

And then I accidentally called him. Dammit, I did not mean to call Omar, but he picked up on the first ring. Just like I knew he would. Dammit, me and my infernal luck !

"Pleased to hear from you, Noor, I'm in class now but I'll call you soon," Omar said in that deep, slightly amused voice of his.

All I could say was a weak "cool" and "bye" before hanging up. Afterwards, I sat there for a long moment, thinking of what I'd just done.

What the hell is it about Omar Augustin that makes me so damn eager to break the rules ? I am NOT like that with males, period. Fuck !

"I so need to pray," I muttered to myself as I made my way to a quiet corner of the library, and did my prayer.

I returned to my seat, and resumed watching the video of Dr. Zakir Naik. Next, I watched a video regarding interracial and intercultural unions in the world of Islam.

In the video, a Somali Muslim man and his Iranian wife talked about the difficulties they ran into, mainly due to her family, as they got together. I watched it intently...

"Oh my," I said to myself, as I watched this Black guy from Somalia and his Iranian wife. As they talked to their interviewer, they smiled and held hands, and even kissed at one point.

I was amazed. In Saudi Arabia, a lot of Arab men have foreign wives and concubines. I've seen Saudi men with African women.

Never thought I'd live to see the day when a Black Muslim man was allowed to marry an Arab woman or a Persian woman. Will wonders never cease ?

I watched the video to completion, and then afterwards, I logged off and headed home. That night, as I lay on my bed, lost in thought, I couldn't shake that image from my head.

Again and again I played the video in my mind, and watched the Somali man and his Persian wife hold hands and kiss.

It got so hot that night that I took off my clothes and slept naked. And I dreamed of the Somali man and his Persian wife, and in my dreams they made love.

Except, for some reason, it wasn't the two of them making love, but myself and Omar. I woke up, screaming and sweaty, utterly disoriented.

I took a few calming breaths. For some reason, my nipples were hard, and my body was sweaty, and I felt a wetness between my legs, followed by a curious tingle.

I touched my vagina, and blinked in surprise upon discovering how wet I was. Omar's face flashed through my mind, further confusing me. Where had those thoughts come from ?

Sometimes, I think that even when the mind doesn't know, or want to acknowledge something, the heart knows.

For long before I fell for Omar, and his charm and wit, and his sweet smile made my heart soar, thoughts of him intruded upon my carefully ordered consciousness.

I couldn't help myself, you see. The Haitian lad had an effect on me...and both my body and my mind were responding to him.

That's how my fascination with Omar Augustin began. I was determined to get to the bottom of this mystery.

Omar and I began to hang out, at first only at school, and then later we ventured into places like the Saint Laurent mall, the Silver City movie theater, and local restaurants like *Soleil Des Iles*, *Creole Sensations* and more.

I discovered Haitian cuisine thanks to that fearless, cocky and wonderful young man, and so much more.

Indeed, Omar changed my life, enriching it in so many ways. The brother was an injection of life into my otherwise dreary existence...

"You're fun company," I said to Omar as we walked out of Silver City, arm in arm, after watching a movie.

It was snowing outside, and I was shivering as Omar and I made our way to the nearby bus station.

I'm a Saudi woman, and I've never seen snow before coming to Canada. I was discovering all kinds of new things, and not all of them were to my liking...

"Right back at you, my dearest Noor, now, if you please, I have a Western tradition to introduce you to," Omar said, smiling slyly.

Shrugging at him, I nodded and adjusted the loose pins in my Hijab as he bent down and picked up a snowball.

I was still fiddling with the pin as he smiled beatifically at me, and then shoved that snowball right in my frigging face...

"Bastard," I cried out, shocked, and I glared murderously at Omar, who stood there, a cocky grin on his dark, handsome face.

I went after him like a missile, and as he tried to flee, I struck him with all of my might. In spite of our size differences, I toppled him.

Indeed, Omar slipped on the freshly fallen snow, and fell. I leapt on top of him, and began to punch
34

him, though I wasn't doing much damage due to his heavy coat...

"Hmm, Miss Saudi Arabia is quite feisty," Omar said, grinning, as I grabbed him by the neck, straddling him, and he held his hands up in mock surrender.

I looked into his eyes, and then, um, something happened. My anger simply melted away, replaced by a curious feeling.

It suddenly occurred to me that I, a Hijab-wearing sister from Saudi Arabia no less, was straddling Omar in the parking lot separating Silver City from the nearby Walmart...

"Shut up, Omar," I all but hissed at him, and then, I grabbed his face, and kissed him. I don't know who was more surprised, myself or Omar.

Like I said, I'm usually quite reserved with the male of the species, for personal and cultural reasons, but Omar, well, the infuriatingly charming Haitian makes me want to do things.

To hell with the consequences, I thought. I kissed Omar, and he wrapped his arms around me and kissed me back.

Thus, Omar and I shared our first kiss, and it was definitely not our last. I surprised myself by allowing myself to be open to the possibility of love, rather than deny myself any chance at happiness by adhering to strict tradition.

My family expected me to graduate from a Canadian University, return to Saudi Arabia, marry a man of their choosing and settle into the life of a housewife and mother.

Well, forgive me for wanting something more. I want to feel alive, and loved, and I want to feel free.

36

In the Kingdom of Saudi Arabia, my beloved and complex homeland, sex and race determine much about one's station in life.

Men are above women over there, for example. A Saudi woman cannot leave the house without a male chaperone, or work without her husband's expressed permission.

And in matters of inheritance, her portion is always smaller than that of her male siblings. And that's just for beginners...

In Canada, I fell in love with Omar Augustin, the young man I call my Habibti. In Saudi Arabia, even if Omar were Muslim as his name seems to suggest, we would not be allowed to be together.

For in my homeland, people of African descent are treated very poorly, and Saudi males and Saudi females treat Blacks with the same contempt.

37

I'm ashamed to say that I held such views until I came to Canada, and met Omar, the young man destined to change my world...

Omar and I walked through the streets of Ottawa, and the venerated halls of Carleton University, hand in hand.

Arabs and others stared at us in open shock, for a lot of Muslims have a die-hard hatred of Africans, even if they pretend to be open-minded and tolerant as far as racial relations go.

Trust me, I know of what I speak. Arab males glared at me with contempt as I smiled lovingly at Omar, and I found the courage not to care...

The way I figure it, we only live once. Someday, perhaps tomorrow, or perhaps many decades from now, I'll be dead.

No force on earth can change that. I just want to live, and be happy for a little while. Forget about tomorrow, and enjoy today.

I wanted to live like a Canadian, be free and be happy, instead of adhering to the strict rules of Saudi culture and my Islamic faith.

I love my Islamic religion, but first and foremost, I'm a human being. I swear, people forget that sometimes. I need to be loved, just like you do...

"You are amazing, my love," Omar said to me, as we lay in bed one night, after making passionate love.

We were at Omar's place, in the east end of Ottawa, and his small apartment has become our sanctuary of sorts.

I lay with my body nestled against his, his strong arms wrapped lovingly around me. Gently Omar

39

kissed me, and then caressed my breasts. I grinned as his hands went to my thick derriere, which he is quite fond of...

"Omar, I'm already in bed, no need to sweet talk me," I replied, and I kissed Omar, and then pushed him down before climbing on top of him.

He looked at me with nothing but love in his eyes, and my heart skipped a beat. Omar's hands went to my breasts, and he pinched my nipples, causing me to giggle.

"Alright, sexy lady," Omar said, and I smiled as he playfully slapped my thick ass, and then his hand slipped between my legs...

"Hmm, so hot," Omar whispered, and he began fingering me, sliding his fingers into my pussy. I licked my lips, for I loved what he was doing to me.

Omar drew me to him, and then he laid me down, spread my legs and then buried his face between my legs.

I closed my eyes, savoring the myriad pleasurable sensations assailing me as Omar licked my pussy and fingered me, and I swear, I was like putty in his hands...

"You're killing me, Habibi," I cried out, squealing in delight as Omar worked his magic on me. As the night rolled on, driven by passion, we tried so many different things together.

I have always been a passionate woman, and aside from a few clandestine encounters with fellow repressed folk of both sexes back in Saudi Arabia, I have rarely had opportunity to explore my sexuality.

With Omar, however, I could finally cut loose and enjoy without being Judged...and the floodgates of passion opened.

"Noor, babe, you haven't felt anything yet," Omar said, grinning as he put me on all fours and spanked my big bum, and I yelped, and giggled.

I love it when he gets rough with me. It's fun, and wonderfully different. Sometimes, though, he can be so gentle it hurts.

I gasped as Omar spread my thick ass cheeks wide open and began eating me out. The feel of his tongue in my asshole as he fingered my pussy is absolutely to die for...

"Now I want to taste you, my sexy man," I said breathlessly to Omar, after he took me to cloud nine, leaving my pussy all tingly thanks to his magic tongue and fingers.

Kneeling before Omar as he sat on the bed, I took his dick into my hands and inhaled his masculine fragrance. Winking at my beloved, I took his dick into my mouth and began sucking on it.

"Easy does it," Omar cooed softly, gently guiding me as I pleasured him orally. I had him right where I wanted him.

I was new to such things, although even among us supposedly cloistered Saudi Arabian Muslim ladies, women share tales of their marital exploits...and lack thereof.

I took my sweet time as I pleasured Omar, and his handsome face was filled with serenity as I made him cum. How to describe the taste of him ? Hmm, simply heavenly, that's for sure.

"Harder," I cried out, much later, as Omar gripped my hips and fucked me silly, as he calls it. Omar

43

took me on all fours, and I went all out, giving myself to him with wild abandon.

My whole body shook under the force of his thrusts as he pulled my hair, spanked my ass and slammed that dick mercilessly into my pussy, leaving me sore in my sweet spot.

Face down and ass up Omar fucked me, and I felt abased but alive. The brother crammed his manhood inside of me, owning me, and I loved it.

"You're like pure fire, Miss Noor, and your King loves you for it," Omar said, much later, as I lay next to him, sweaty and exhausted, and reeking of my own womanly juices.

With him, I felt no fear or shame. For when Omar looks at me, I feel as though I'm the most beautiful woman in the world.

I grew up feeling that the female body was a curse, and that men had to be protected from it. Omar showed me that I'm beautiful, and in his eyes, almost akin to perfection...

"I love you Omar," I whispered, and then I kissed him. Omar kissed me back, and whispered into my ear how much he loved me.

Pulling the covers over our spent, pleasurably sore bodies, my dear Omar hit the lights and then began to sleep.

Lying next to him, I felt safe and happy. Happier than I'd ever been, in fact. I felt as though my soul were soaring the halls of Jannah.

Omar treated me better than any man I'd ever met. And I've lived on two continents. So why was I weeping ? Tears of joy, they get to you...

"I want to be with you always," Omar said to me one day, after we'd dined at *Rooster's Café*, a chic little restaurant located on the fourth floor of the University Center Building at Carleton.

Sitting at our favorite table, right by the window overlooking the Atrium, we were at peace, dining on tasty egg sandwiches and washing them down with Pepsis.

"I'm with you now, handsome," I replied, smiling at Omar as I took a sip of my Pepsi. At this hour, the restaurant was getting crowded.

The patrons reflected the diversity and liveliness of the Carleton campus. I saw a young Somali guy with his blonde-haired White girlfriend place their order, and someone stared daggers at them.

Indeed, a chubby White guy with his Asian girlfriend shot them a strange look as he and his date sat nearby.

That, to me, is a reflection of Ottawa at its best. I had a pretty good idea of what was going on inside the chubby White guy's mind.

Even though he is in interracial relationship, what with his girlfriend being Asian and all, he wasn't thrilled to see a Black man from Somalia with one of his precious White women.

Hypocrisy without fear or shame. See ? That's Canada for you. I swear, there's always a bit of tension under the multiculturalism stuff that they peddle left and right...

"Noor, we're both going to graduate soon, well, I was hoping that you'd stay in Ottawa after," Omar said, and I bit my lip and looked at him.

47

Clad in a Black leather jacket over a blue silk shirt, Black silk pants and dark red tie, Omar looked dashingly handsome.

Recently, Omar started working as a teacher's assistant to make some extra money and I couldn't be prouder of him. My man is going to go far...

"Omar, you know I love you, Habibi, but I have to return to Saudi Arabia after I graduate," I said softly, answering Omar at last while linking my hand with his.

Omar looked at my hand, and then stared at me, a spooked expression on his handsome face. I looked away for a moment, then fixed my gaze on him.

Omar shook his head, and pursed his lips, something he only did when he was about to say something he found difficult to say...

"Noor, I love you, but I hate it when you lie to yourself, there's nothing for you in Saudi Arabia except misery and pain, you are getting a Canadian University degree, you should stay here and have a life and a career, instead of going back there to be little more than a slave for some random guy so wrapped up in tradition he can't see you for the amazing woman you are," Omar said hotly, and I smiled faintly, moved by his words, though they stung a bit.

"It's not that easy, Omar, I love my life in Canada and our school, but I have to go back to Saudi Arabia, my family is there, and I couldn't stay in Canada even if I wanted to, I'm not a citizen or a permanent resident," I countered, looking right at him.

I gazed into Omar's soulful eyes and hoping that somehow, I could make him see reason. Omar

49

sighed deeply and took my hands in his, and kissed them gently.

"Noor, is it because I'm not Muslim ? I'll convert, and then we'll be together, I have grown to respect Islam as I discovered it while seeing you, I love you and your faith, and besides, I'd still be worshiping the same Creator," Omar said, smiling hopefully.

I smiled, touched by Omar's candor and his willingness to change his ways, just for me. I would never ask him that, of course.

"Omar, I cherish you, and you've enriched my life in so many ways, this has nothing to do with religion," I said, and a look of confusion crept into Omar's handsome face.

I could almost see the wheels turning in that sharp mind of his. What a beautiful young man, I thought.

A woman could travel across a thousand lifetimes without finding such a man...and here one was, sitting across from me.

"Noor, I'm a Canadian citizen by birth, if you stay, I'll sponsor you and you can get your permanent residency that way, we'll be together, and everything will be alright, I'll take care of you," Omar said, and I looked at him and smiled, and then kissed him on the lips.

My heart thundered in my chest, and all the love and affection I felt for this rambunctious and fearless young Haitian-Canadian threatened to burst forth like water out of a damn...

"Omar, I love you more than anything, and I wish I could stay in Canada, and be your wife, and bear you as many sons and daughters as you want, but my place is in the Kingdom of Saudi Arabia," I said firmly, once we came up for air.

Omar looked at me and flinched as though he'd been slapped. There was a look of raw, almost elemental pain on his handsome face.

I felt as though someone had thrust a blade through my chest. It hurt me so much to see Omar in pain, and to know that I was the cause of it...

"You're wrong, Noor, what we have is special, and I wish you wouldn't throw it away out of loyalty to outdated stupid traditions," Omar said, his ire rising.

Several patrons sitting nearby looked at us, and one of the female servers at the *Rooster's Café* counter tilted her head to one side inquisitively.

I smiled reassuringly at them, wishing to high heaven that my beloved Omar wouldn't cause a damn scene...

"Omar, please," I pleaded with him, and Omar looked at me, smiled sadly and vigorously shook his head.

"I can't do this," Omar said. Rising from his chair, my boo stood in front of me, and I looked up at him.

My majestic Haitian prince and the only person in this world who has ever truly loved me without measure.

Omar bent low and gently kissed me on the forehead, and then, over my protests, my tall, dark and handsome prince walked away.

And I'm ashamed to say that I did not go after him. I remained rooted to my chair, unable to frigging move.

Over the next few months, my existence reverted to its dreary state. I was still attending classes at Carleton University, and still living in the City of Ottawa.

I still went to the movies, and enjoyed activities with the Muslim Scholars Association, the biggest club at school.

I missed Omar, whom I still loved deeply, but he wasn't talking to me. When we ran into each other at school, he was polite but distant. As if I were a mere acquaintance of his or something.

I remember bristling with jealousy and raw anger the first time I saw Omar walking around with someone else.

I was coming out of the University Center Building's women's washroom when I saw Omar walking around with someone.

A tall, chubby and big-bottomed, fake-smiling and blonde-haired White chick whom I recognized as Janice something or other, from the International Student Office.

Omar's eyes met mine, and Janice followed his gaze. I swear the bitch smiled. Fuming, I looked away and walked in the opposite direction.

"So that's how it ends," I said to myself, lamenting the end of my relationship with Omar Augustin. I shall definitely miss him.

55

I will miss our outings to our favorite places like Soleil Des Iles, Creole Sensations, the Silver City movie theater, and the National Gallery of Canada.

I'll miss our long romantic walks, hand in hand, as we walked through Hog's Back Park. Our history is written all over Ottawa, and losing all that was quite painful to me...

Time went by, and I graduated from Carleton University with my bachelor's degree in Business Administration.

My parents, Afaf Alzahrani and Mohammed Alzahrani flew in from Saudi Arabia, to watch my big moment.

I graduated with honors, and I had tears of joy and pain in my eyes as I clutched my degree in my hand.

I embraced my smiling parents and then resolved to return to Saudi Arabia and embrace the next chapter of my life.

As far as I was concerned, Omar Augustin, Carleton University and the City of Ottawa had become part of my past...

At least, that's what I told myself. I thought I could forget about Omar Augustin and our lost world, the Carleton University campus, our favorite malls, restaurants and movie theaters.

I thought I could will myself to let go of the most wonderful time of my life and embrace my homeland, with all of its wonders and horrors.

There's no place like home, as they say. I quite stubbornly refused to believe that I had changed so much that home wasn't home anymore...

"Welcome home, my dear," said my Baba, Mohammed Ali, as I set foot on the family estate in the beautiful Al-Faisal neighborhood of metropolitan Riyadh's Eastern Quarter.

I looked at the two-story, five-bedroom, walled villa in which I grew up and smiled. I hadn't seen it in ages, and had missed it sorely.

I embraced my father and mother, and returned to my bedroom. I didn't even bother unpacking. I lay on my bed, and smiled. It was good to finally be home...

Not long after I returned home, my parents began to talk of marriage. Nothing out of the ordinary there.

After all, I was a lovely, educated young Saudi Arabian Muslim woman from a good family, and I also happen to be the holder of a Canadian University degree.

My parents searched, and then finally found what they thought to be a suitable candidate for making an honest woman out of me.

Ibrahim Al-Shehri, a tall, handsome young Saudi Arabian Muslim man originally from Dammam, in the Eastern Province.

This young man studied Civil Engineering at the University of Michigan, and graduated with highest honors.

When he came back to Saudi Arabia, he found work with *Qadir Tech*, one of the top companies in the Riyadh region.

For some reason, my folks thought we'd be a good match merely based on the fact that we both studied abroad, go figure...

"I'm glad to be home, with my own people, I missed Saudi Arabia so much, and Saudi Arabian women most of all, those Western women are vile and uncouth, a bunch of she-devils," Ibrahim Al-Shehri said, laughing merrily, as he and his parents dined with my family and I.

Frowning, I looked at Ibrahim, and recalled thinking that I found him handsome and charming until he opened his mouth and said those utterly stupid things about Western women...

"Brother Ibrahim, our daughter Noor is a good woman, a pious and studious sister, nothing like those Western women with loose morals," Baba replied, and Ibrahim nodded and smiled, then I forced a smile.

All of a sudden, I felt like leaving. I couldn't frigging breathe. Excusing myself I left the table, and went out on the balcony.

Smoking a cigarette, something I hadn't done in ages since Omar got me to quit, I quietly fumed about my parents, Ibrahim's words, and the whole situation...

All of a sudden, I felt trapped in the family estate in Riyadh, and truth be told, I knew in my soul that returning to the Kingdom of Saudi Arabia had been a mistake.

Listening to my Baba and Ibrahim talk, I felt sick to my stomach. I love my family, but after living in Ottawa, and seeing how fearless the women over there are, I've outgrown Saudi Arabia.

The Kingdom of Saudi Arabia hadn't changed at all but against all odds, I actually have, in ways I never could have predicted...

I overlooked a lot of things about Saudi Arabian society due to my nostalgia and homesickness, and I made a mistake.

I missed my life in Ottawa sorely. I saw female soldiers giving orders to male soldiers when Omar took me on a tour of the Canadian Forces Base in the City of Trenton, Ontario.

I saw female police officers arrest male suspects who'd gotten into drunken brawls at the Rideau Shopping Center.

In the Ontario province of Canada, where I used to live, women are fearless. In Saudi Arabia, men rule and women obey. What a dichotomy...

"Be a proper wife to me, Noor, and everything will be fine," Ibrahim Al-Shehri said to me, on our wedding night, as he drew me to our marriage bed.

His parents, Wahabi preacher Nasser Al-Shehri gifted us with a beautiful villa just outside the City of Riyadh.

This was my wedding night, the night every woman has dreamt off since time immemorial, and I was not a happy bride.

Indeed, I felt trepidation and a hint of dread rather than excitement. In spite of my reservations, I went through with it.

"I will do my best," I replied as Ibrahim Al-Shehri kissed me, and then he laid me on the bed and took me.

Ibrahim did not caress me, or please me. He did not kiss my lips or lick my breasts. He did not lick

63

my pussy. Instead he spread my legs, and shoved his dick into me.

Ibrahim Al-Shehri, my new husband, did not make love to me. He fucked me, pure and simple. And I did not enjoy it.

Not after the intense, romantic-yet-rough, passionate lovemaking I'd enjoyed thanks to my beloved Omar Augustin.

At first, things were pleasant enough between my new husband Ibrahim Al-Shehri and myself. We had a lovely home, and servants.

Ibrahim gave me a monthly stipend, the Saudi equivalent of two thousand Canadian dollars. I had a driver and a limo, and went out to shop a lot.

I got to know the other housewives in the neighborhood. Things were tranquil, and then the shit hit the fan.

64

I made Ibrahim mad when I disapproved of his dalliance with Rosa, one of the Filipina female servants attached to our household.

"Noor, I see that life in Canada has given you a sassy mouth, I won't tolerate that," Ibrahim Al-Shehri shouted, right before he struck me.

I gaped at him, astonished. Shrugging, he walked away, shaking his head. With tears in my eyes, I went to the mirror, and blinked at the bruises on my face.

Shaking my head, I closed my eyes, hard. After washing my face, I returned to my library and kept out of his way until Ibrahim left for work.

"Ignoble brute," I said angrily, watching as Ibrahim Al-Shehri, my brute of a husband drove away in his bright red Mercedes convertible.

That's when it dawned on me what a colossal mistake I'd made. Omar Augustin was poor, and hard-working, and he treated me like a goddess.

Not once did he ever mistreat me in any way. Ibrahim is wealthy and powerful, and treats me like a possession. Oh, and he hits me. I'd chosen the wrong man...

One night, after Ibrahim Al-Shehri beat me, took me by force and then fell asleep after sating his lustful desires, I got up and went to the kitchen.

Withdrawing a knife from a drawer, I marched to the bedroom, where my erstwhile husband Ibrahim slept peacefully.

Without hesitation I plunged the blade into his chest. Again and again I stabbed him, ignoring his cries of pain and pleas for mercy.

66

I did not stop until Ibrahim Al-Shehri was dead as a doornail. When the police came, they found with the bloody knife still in my hand.

Sleeping on my cot in my prison cell, so far away from the City of Ottawa, Carleton University and Omar's apartment, I smiled with satisfaction.

I did not regret slaying Ibrahim Al-Shehri. Nor did I waste time thinking about him. Erotic thoughts of Omar and his sturdy, muscular and dark-skinned body haunt my troubled mind.

I miss his kisses, and the feel of his skin, and the smell of his body as we make love. I was a fool to leave Omar and Ottawa behind.

I wish I were far away from Saudi Arabia, the forsaken place where I first saw the light of day, and the place where, apparently, I will die...

"I love you my sweet Omar," I whisper as I look out the window. Our nights of love are something I will hold dear until the day I die. Which isn't too far off, by the way.

Today is indeed Jummah, or Friday. In a few hours, I will be marched to Deera Square in central Riyadh, also known as "Chop-Chop Square."

It's where the public executions of condemned men and women are carried out, usually in front of huge crowds. A Saudi Arabian special, ladies and gentlemen.

I close my eyes, and think of another time and place, and how different my life might have been if I had chosen to remain in Ottawa with Omar, and become his wife and bore him sons and daughters.

I would have been happy to share my life with him, but instead I bowed to tradition, and faith, and culture, and broke his heart.

I returned to Saudi Arabia, determined to be true to my heritage even though its draconian rules are definitely a soul killer...

My last year in the City of Ottawa were filled with great pleasure and immense turmoil, as you can imagine.

I savored every moment I spent with Omar, partly because I was madly in love with the guy, and partly because I knew that it was coming to an end.

The fabric of fate has already been written long before any of us draw our first breath in this world.

People need to realize the truth of that. I already have. Life happens, and there's very little any of us can do...

I had a dream once. I'll share it with you since, well, who else am I going to tell ? In my dream, I walked away from my old life in the Kingdom of Saudi Arabia and stayed in Ottawa.

Omar Augustin proposed to me and I accepted, and we began building a life together in the Canadian Capital.

One day, feeling a bit sickly, I went to the nearby *Appletree Medical Clinic*, and the doctor told me that I was pregnant. Overjoyed, I rushed home to share the news with my husband Omar.

"Masha' Allah, this is wonderful news," Omar Augustin said, and my husband, who by now was sporting a full beard and wearing a Kufi hat, swept me into his arms and kissed me.

I kissed Omar back passionately, and grinned as he knelt before me and kissed my belly. For within me I carried the fruit of our love, a son or daughter who would be the first of their kind.

Half Haitian and half Saudi Arabian, and one hundred percent Canadian. The offspring of unique parents.

"You're going to make an awesome Baba (daddy) when the time comes," I whisper to Omar, and we kiss again.

Sniffing, I closed my eyes hard, as I awakened to grim reality on the last morning of my life. What I dreamt of could never be and it's all my fault.

I chose to return to Saudi Arabia and marry Ibrahim Al-Shehri, and now I've been branded a killer, and tried and convicted by the merciless Royal Judiciary of Saudi Arabia.

I should be far away, in a much better and more humane nation, but this is the path that I've chosen.

In the Western world, even in America, where there's a death penalty, I could have used the battered woman's defense in court, and perhaps gotten clemency.

My case did make headlines around the world, and organizations like *Human Rights Watch* and *Amnesty International* even contacted the Saudi Arabian government on my behalf, but to no avail...

I wonder what Omar Augustin and my Canadian friends thought when they found out what had happened to me...

Even if I could have done things differently, it's most definitely much too late to matter one bit now...

"See you in Jannah, my sweet Omar," I say to him, visualizing my tall, dark and handsome Black Canadian stud in my mind's eye one last time.

My last day upon this earth passes very quickly. It's all so damn short, when your time comes, doesn't it ?

Jummah Prayers are over. The crowds spill forth from the Masjids, the shops, the restaurants, the museums and the cyber cafes.

The officers come to my door, and I am allowed one last prayer before I am marched to Deera Square.

The executioner, an infamous Saudi man who once sat down with *The Guardian* newspaper to discuss

73

his passion for his rather gruesome work, awaits me.

Like the Angel of Death, the masked executioner awaits. Everyone in Saudi Arabian society knows what he looks like, why does he hide his face ?

I wonder what goes through the mind of a man like that. Day in and day out, you get paid to slaughter other people.

How do you live with yourself ? Does that man have nightmares about what he does or is he fine with it ?

When I approach the place of my death, I am expected to struggle, and beg for mercy. A condemned person's strength tends to drain away in their final moments...

A crowd of onlookers has gathered to watch me die. I have become infamous in Saudi society, for I am the rebellious woman who murdered her husband for punishing her for having Western ways...

Like a pig about to be slaughtered, I am expected to make one final, desperate act of resistance or defiance.

I will not give the two-faced dregs of Saudi Arabian society the pleasure of a spectacle. I don't even struggle as I am brought forth.

That's when the crowd of onlookers starts to cheer. They're thrilled to see a hapless woman about to be executed. Savages !

Don't let these filthy excuses for human beings see you cry, I tell myself, and I steel myself for the horror that is upon me.

I close my eyes as I am brought to my knees, and visualize Omar's arms around me, and his lips pressed against mine.

A prince of a man in a world of mindless brutes. I should have married him. *See you in the next world.* I smile sadly, and the blade falls. Darkness greets me.

UNDER THE NEPEAN SUN

"Zeinab Al-Suwaiyel, you do not at the present time meet the *Immigration & Refugee Board's* Criteria and Conditions for refugee protection, therefore, your request for political asylum has been denied," read the letter from *Citizenship & Immigration Canada*, and Zeinab Al-Suwaiyel shook her head, and sighed deeply.

This was the end of all hope for her. Having denied her refugee claim, the Canadian government would be coming for her.

They were sure to send Zeinab back to Saudi Arabia, where her cruel ex-husband and family awaited, with vengeance on their minds.

The young Saudi Arabian Muslim woman's heart thundered in her chest, and she exhaled sharply, willing herself to be calm.

So this is how it ends, Zeinab thought, and she crumpled the letter into a ball and tossed it into the trash can.

After living in the Capital region of Canada for years and years, Zeinab was starting to think of it as home. After all, she had a job she loved, and friends.

And recently, she'd begun taking classes at Algonquin College. To the Canadian government, her hopes and dreams apparently meant absolutely nothing...

Lying on her bed, in the one-bedroom spot she rented on Canter Boulevard in the suburb of Nepean, Ontario, Zeinab closed her eyes.

Since Zeinab moved to the Canadian Capital from her hometown of Al-Jubayl, Saudi Arabia, life had been a rollercoaster ride at best.

Zeinab first set foot in the City of Ottawa, Ontario, in the summer of 2013, with her then-husband Hamid Alharbi.

They were on their honeymoon, and everything was wonderful. And then Zeinab discovered a side to Hamid that she never knew existed...

"Habibi, this City of Ottawa is so beautiful, I'd love to stay here if you do end up setting up a new business in town," Zeinab said excitedly as she walked through Parliament Hill with her new hubby Hamid.

"You'd like to stay here, huh ? I don't think it's a good idea, I'm told that here, even our Arab sisters dress like whores, just like the Whites," Hamid said, and he cut his eyes at a tall, red-haired White woman who walked by in a short skirt and tank top.

"Hamid, my love, we've only been in Canada for a couple of weeks, we shouldn't Judge these people," Zeinab said cautiously.

The young Saudi woman looked at a couple of uniformed policewomen, one tall, athletic and dark-skinned, the other stout and blonde-haired, as they walked by.

"They have female police in this country? They even let African women be police up here? Fascinating, the Whites have truly gone mad," Hamid said, his lip curled in distaste.

Hamid had seen the two policewomen and was not impressed. And he didn't notice the way his wife's eyes lit up upon seeing them.

"Amazing," Zeinab whispered to herself, and the young woman smiled. In her homeland of Saudi Arabia, female soldiers and female officers were unheard of.

It would seem that what the clerics warned them about in their sermons against Western excess and strangeness was true.

"I could be a policewoman here, if we end up staying," Zeinab said jokingly to Hamid, who shot her a look.

In Western society, women could do pretty much anything they wanted, and there was very little that males could do to stop them.

"I think Western ideas are already starting to infect you, you're going home with me and that's final, you're nothing without me," Hamid chastised Zeinab.

Hamid had been incensed after Zeinab strongly hinted to him that she liked the idea of settling down in the City of Ottawa.

After all, Hamid had done a lot of business in the Toronto area and thought about expanding to the City of Ottawa.

Zeinab had fallen in love with the Canadian Capital during their trip, and found herself dreaming of a life there, but her husband did not share that sentiment.

"As you wish," Zeinab replied, using a deferential tone with her husband Hamid Alharbi, as was customary in their homeland.

That night, as Zeinab lay in bed next to her husband Hamid Alharbi, she thought of the events of the day.

"I've gone and married the wrong man," Zeinab whispered to herself, and she looked at Hamid's slumbering silhouette with sadness.

On the day she was supposed to join her wealthy businessman hubby at the Ottawa International Airport, Zeinab fled their rented townhouse with only the clothes on her back.

Hamid had her passport and without it, Zeinab knew her options were severely limited. Nevertheless, Zeinab refused to look back.

Thus the forlorn young woman began her journey in this strange, wonderful and at times rough country called Canada.

"I'd rather live on a tiny cot than to share a palace with a man who treats me like shit," Zeinab said to Nancy Vernet, the young French Canadian social worker at the social services office on Constellation Road, not far from the Algonquin College campus.

Nancy looked at Zeinab with sincere empathy in her eyes, and then nodded gently. Her demeanor was not what Zeinab expected.

For some reason, this blonde-haired, twenty-something White woman seemed to relate to Zeinab's pain, much to her surprise.

83

"I used to date a bastard named Bill who liked to treat me like this, I know how you feel, Zeinab, I'll do whatever I can to help you," Nancy Vernet said firmly, and Zeinab looked at her and nodded gratefully.

That same afternoon, Zeinab went to the nearby RBC Bank and sat down with an account manager to set up a checking account.

With Nancy's help, Zeinab was also able to get an Ontario Photo ID Card, a necessity since she didn't have any other forms of identification.

"I will survive," Zeinab said to herself, as she thought of the incredible twists and turns her life had taken.

Hamid Alharbi returned to Al Jubayl, Saudi Arabia, with Zeinab's passport and informed her via Facebook that he'd destroyed it.

84

Oh, and Hamid also divorced his runaway bride in absentia. Zeinab was now stranded in the City of Ottawa, without any friends or family, or any means of support.

Nevertheless, the young Saudi Arabian Muslim woman was determined to build a life for herself in the Canadian Capital.

Nancy Vernet proved to be a tremendous help for Zeinab. She helped her get a work permit, and with it, a social insurance card.

With those documents, Zeinab walked into the Tim Horton's located in her neighborhood and applied for a job.

The restaurant manager, a tall, forty-something Black man named Mustapha Klassou, hired her on the spot.

Thus, Zeinab got herself a job and a place to stay. For once things went right. It was her first victory in a long, rough time...

"What's wrong, Zeinab ?" Mustapha asked her, when Zeinab walked in that afternoon, a forlorn look on her lovely face.

Mustapha looked at Zeinab, and was surprised to see tears brimming in her eyes. *This won't do*, he thought.

Standing only five-foot-seven, a bit chubby, with dark bronze skin and curly dark hair which she always tucked away under her Hijab, Zeinab was nevertheless one of the strongest women that Mustapha knew.

Mustapha recalled that time when a racist White customer had been giving him a hard time, and Zeinab stepped in and told him off...

86

"Listen, buddy, if you don't stop harassing my co-workers, I will call the police and say that you were about to commit a hate crime, and I'll make sure it sticks to you," Zeinab haughtily said to the irate customer.

Locking eyes with him, Zeinab stood her ground. The angry customer, a middle-aged, balding White guy with reddish brown hair looked at the short, round little Saudi Arabian woman who stood before him, her brown eyes blazing with anger.

Indeed, he looked like he wanted to say something, but everyone inside the Tim Horton's was watching...

"Fucking immigrants," Mr. Angry Man said, and he walked out of the Tim Horton's, shoving his way past a few people who were standing in line.

After the bozo left, a lot of people stood up and applauded Zeinab, and the young Saudi woman smiled and nodded.

Mustapha, who had been stunned when the angry old White dude got on his case because he had three sugars instead of five in his coffee, sighed in relief.

"You're totally my hero, Zeinab," Mustapha said, and Zeinab smiled and nodded, then patted him on the shoulder.

Mustapha found that gesture comforting but also surprising. Muslim women, especially the ones from the ultra-conservative realm of Saudi Arabia, were a touch-me-not club.

Zeinab on the other hand was very friendly, outgoing and oddly affectionate. And he was quite fond of her.

More than he cared to admit. That's why seeing her come in with teary eyes bothered Mustapha so much...

"They're going to kill me if the Canadian government sends me back to Saudi Arabia," Zeinab said, and she handed the crumpled piece of paper to Mustapha, who unfolded it and read it.

After he finished reading the letter, Mustapha looked at her with sympathy, but he wasn't sure what to say.

Zeinab smiled and shrugged, and then resumed pouring coffee for an impatient-looking young White woman with hair dyed bright pink.

What a woman, Mustapha thought, admiring Zeinab's calm demeanor. Could he have managed to do as much under those circumstances ?

Mustapha thought of his own path in Canada, which was far from easy. Born in the City of Lome, Capital of the West African nation of Togo, Mustapha Klassou came to Canada in 1997 at the age of nineteen.

Political unrest drove him and his parents, Ahmed Klassou and Nina Eyadema-Klassou, to come to Canada to claim refugee status.

Fortunately in those days, the Canadian government was lenient toward foreigners, and accepted the Klassou family's claim.

Mustapha Klassou enrolled at the University of Ottawa, where he studied Business Management, graduating with his MBA in the summer of 2003.

In 2004, Mustapha began working as a Business Development Manager for the Department of Public

Works, a position he held until his firing in the summer of 2013.

Try as he might, Mustapha couldn't find another job in the government or the private sector. Someone Blacklisted him in the Canadian professional classes, it would seem.

That's how Mustapha ended up as a manager at the Tim Horton's where he met and subsequently hired and befriended Zeinab Al-Suwaiyel.

"Don't despair my friend, we'll find a way to save you," Mustapha said to Zeinab as the two of them grabbed lunch at *Quizno's* restaurant on their break.

Zeinab looked at Mustapha and flashed him a brave smile. The tall, dark and handsome Togolese-Canadian Muslim gentleman wasn't just her boss.

Mustapha was also one of the friendliest and most compassionate people she knew. Oh, and a good Muslim as well.

Zeinab recalled how Mustapha let her use his mailing address several times over the years, since she moved around a lot. If only...

"Thanks for your kind words, brother," Zeinab replied, gently brushing her hand against Mustapha's.

In her homeland of Saudi Arabia, Zeinab watched her fellow Arabs treat Africans very poorly and it always bothered her.

In Ottawa, Zeinab got to know many Africans from a variety of nations and found them to be friendly, decent and hard-working people.

If not for Mustapha's support, Zeinab knew that she wouldn't have made it this far. When she needed help finding a lawyer, Mustapha convinced his cousin Ibrahim Klassou to represent her.

Mustapha was indeed a wonder. The man was so kind, and handsome too. Zeinab was not oblivious to his charms.

Living in Canada, having to work for her own survival rather than depending on a husband like most women back in Saudi Arabia did, Zeinab began to change.

The young Saudi woman gained knowledge about the world and about herself. One thing she knew for sure, is that a good man is a rare find...

Mustapha looked at Zeinab, and seemed like he was about to say something when something caught his attention.

Zeinab followed his gaze and saw a tall, handsome and well-dressed Black guy walk into the Quizno's restaurant, hand in hand with a tall, busty White woman with blonde hair and a big butt.

Life in Ottawa taught Zeinab to get used to interracial couples, which were rare in Saudi Arabian society.

"What is it with brothers and women with big butts ?" Zeinab said slyly, and she playfully slapped Mustapha's hand, causing the Togolese brother to snap out of his reverie.

Mustapha blushed and smiled bashfully. This wasn't the first time that Zeinab caught him checking out another female.

If Mustapha had a weakness it was big-bottomed women. He simply couldn't resist them, and no one knew this better than Zeinab...

"I'm sorry, I got, um, distracted," Mustapha said, and Zeinab grinned and rolled her eyes. Excusing herself to go to the washroom, Zeinab 'accidentally' dropped her pen, and bent down to pick it up.

When she briefly turned around, she could see Mustapha's eyes on her. Of course he'd checked out her bottom, just like Zeinab knew he would...

"So, boss, did you get a good look when I bent down? And most importantly, is my butt bigger than hers?" Zeinab said in a conspirator-like way as she sat back down.

Mustapha looked at her, stunned, and Zeinab smiled. The Togolese Muslim brother was always surprised when Zeinab dropped the wallflower act and spoke her mind.

She wasn't shy, soft and sweet like so many of the Arab ladies he knew. Nope, Zeinab was definitely one of a kind...

"Um, well, oh my, I don't know what to say, Zeinab," Mustapha said, shocked by her words and coy demeanor.

Zeinab smiled and that's when Mustapha gasped. For she'd reached under the table and laid her hand on his thigh.

Yes, in that spot. Mustapha flinched, then smiled nervously. Looking at the curvy, Hijab-wearing Saudi beauty who sat opposite him, he was mesmerized.

For Mustapha saw a burning desire in Zeinab's eyes, and a come-hither look. Time for a brother to bust a move, as they say...

"So don't say anything," Zeinab said, smiling as Mustapha finally grew a pair and drew closer to her, until his dark, handsome face was inches from hers.

That's when he manned up and kissed her. Zeinab kissed Mustapha back, and he slid his tongue into her mouth.

As patrons in nearby tables looked on, the tall Togolese brother and the curvy young Saudi woman made out like it was nobody's business.

When they came up for air, they smiled at each other. Happy as can be...and oblivious to their surroundings.

"You have sweet lips," Mustapha said, smiling at Zeinab, who nodded eagerly. Shortly after, they left the restaurant, hand in hand.

Mustapha did several things that were out of character that day. He called his assistant manager, Sophie, and told her he'd be leaving early.

As for Zeinab, she texted Sophie to inform her of an undisclosed emergency. Grinning, Zeinab and

Mustapha walked down Baseline Road, and headed for her place on Canter Boulevard.

"I've been wanting to do this for so long," Zeinab said, as she sat Mustapha down, and undressed before him.

Mustapha sat on a nearby chair, his eyes riveted on Zeinab as the young woman disrobed, revealing her curvaceous loveliness.

The bronze-skinned, wide-hipped and large-breasted, big-bottomed gal stood before him, stark naked and looking glorious. *Such beauty*, Mustapha thought admiringly.

"You are so beautiful," Mustapha whispered, and a smiling Zeinab walked up to him. Drawing her into his arms, Mustapha kissed her full and deep, and then Zeinab lovingly wrapped herself around him.

For ages he'd dreamed of her, such a beautiful and lively woman, and now, at last, they were about to drink each other in. Mustapha stroked Zeinab's lovely face, and she smiled and sucked on his thumb.

"Make love to me," Zeinab said softly, and Mustapha saw a burning desire and a command in her eyes.

Laying her on the bed, he kissed her lips and caressed her breasts, pinching the areolas. Zeinab sighed happily as Mustapha began pleasuring her.

The Togolese Muslim brother definitely knew his way around the female body, and this gladdened Zeinab's heart.

Pleasure-filled groans erupted from Zeinab as Mustapha spread her thick thighs and began licking her pussy. It had been so long since she'd known a man's touch...

"You taste amazing," Mustapha paused to say, as he lathered up Zeinab's pussy with his tongue, and teased her clit with his nimble fingers.

Zeinab squealed in delight, driven absolutely wild by what Mustapha was doing to her. To really shine her on, Mustapha switched things up.

Zeinab grinned as Mustapha propped her on all fours and caressed her big bronze booty, then spread her ass cheeks wide open.

"Oh yes, eat my ass," Zeinab squealed, arching her back as Mustapha playfully slapped her thick bum. Inhaling the smell of her booty, Mustapha slid his tongue into her asshole and began to pleasure her that way.

This was hot, forbidden, and intimate. Zeinab simply couldn't get enough of it, as Mustapha licked her ass with passion.

Mustapha fingered her pussy as he tongued her asshole, and she was like putty in his agile hands, moaning and crying out his name.

"That is fantastic," Mustapha said, licking his lips as he watched Zeinab shudder violently, orgasmic thanks to his endless licking and probing of her holes.

Zeinab sighed happily once the sensations wracking her voluptuous, horny body subsided. Mustapha truly rocked her world.

The young woman looked up at her lover, and grinned, thankful beyond measure for what he'd done to her. And for her.

Zeinab's eyes flitted up and down Mustapha's body, zeroing in on his crotch, and she licked her lips lustfully.

"My turn to please you, handsome, now lie down and relax, Habibi," Zeinab said softly, and Mustapha grinned as she grabbed his dick and stroked it.

Instantly he hardened, and smiled upon realizing how wrong he'd been about Zeinab. Indeed, the young Saudi woman straddled him, and pumped her hands up and down the length of his shaft.

Zeinab looked at Mustapha hungrily, and he watched, amazed, as she leaned over and took him into her mouth...

"Damn it, you are freaky, you crazy beautiful woman," Mustapha whispered, and Zeinab paused, winked at him and then flicked her tongue over his dick head.

Slowly, lovingly, Zeinab sucked Mustapha's dick and tugged on his ball sac. She worked him over real good, and soon he found himself throbbing.

Once Zeinab had Mustapha good and hard, Zeinab looked at him, and tugged on his dick as he sat up. Zeinab licked her lips, an expectant look on her lovely face...

"Let's see what you're made of," Zeinab said, grinning mischievously as she pushed Mustapha down on the bed and straddled him.

Mustapha smiled and caressed Zeinab's tits with one hand and playfully slapped her big round ass with the other.

Zeinab grinned, and rubbed Mustapha's dick against her pussy. There was a fire at her core, and only he could put it out. If he was up to the task, that is...

"Challenge accepted, Miss Zeinab, now, come ride this Jimmy," Mustapha said, and Zeinab smiled at the moniker he used for his penis.

Without further ado, Zeinab impaled herself on Mustapha's dick, sighing deeply as his hard dick filled her up.

"Shut up and fuck me," Zeinab hissed as Mustapha bucked his hips and thrust into her, and she began to ride him, hard.

Zeinab welcomed the deliciously hot pain she felt down below as Mustapha's dick invaded her pussy, exploring womanly folds that hadn't been probed or pleasured in ages...

"Pull my hair and fuck me harder," Zeinab squealed, pressing her big ass against Mustapha's groin as he took her from behind.

Hard and fast he pumped his dick into her snatch, which gripped his dick like a vise. Mustapha went to town on Zeinab, smacking her big ass which jiggled under the force of his thrusts.

Grabbing a fistful of her long dark hair, which was Hijab-free for a change, Mustapha yanked Zeinab's head back and spanked her big ass as he fucked her.

"Dammit, Zeinab, you're going to break my dick," Mustapha laughed, as Zeinab rolled off of him, after they'd been going at it for several hours.

Zeinab grinned and lay beside him on her small bed, and the two lovebirds exchanged another passionate kiss.

Lying in bed with Mustapha, in a tiny room in a crowded Canadian suburb, Zeinab Al-Suwaiyel felt happy for the first time in ages.

Astonishing how it took losing everything to make Zeinab realize what truly mattered, though she was glad to have gained such an interesting retrospective.

Zeinab thought of her old life in Al-Jubayl, Saudi Arabia, and of her former husband and family. Her feelings toward her homeland and the people she left behind were always complicated.

Saudi Arabia flowed through her veins and would always be part of her, but she had to admit that her life was now in the City of Ottawa.

Perhaps, by the Grace of the Most High, the fates would let her build a life in the Canadian Capital, who knows ?

"Hmm, Mustapha, I thank you for making me feel alive," Zeinab said, gently stroking Mustapha's dark, handsome face.

The Togolese Muslim brother smiled and gently rubbed his index finegr against Zeinab's full lips. It was astonishing how much he cared for this vivacious, lively young woman from the other side of the world.

Prior to meeting Zeinab, Mustapha thought Arab women forever unreachable and haughty, almost like the stars in the night sky in a way.

The woman who lay in his arms was very real, very lovely and very vulnerable, though she put up quite a brave face...

"Right back at you, Zeinab, this wasn't just sex for me, I care for you," Mustapha said, and Zeinab looked into his eyes, and smiled.

They kissed again, and for the rest of the afternoon, they were constantly together. They went out for a walk, grabbed ice cream and hopped on the bus.

Returning home, they ordered Chinese food, ate, and then made love before falling asleep in each other's arms.

To many more fun and passionate days like this one, Zeinab thought as she rested her head against Mustapha's chest.

Thus began a most remarkable and game-changing chapter in Zainab Al-Suwaiyel and Mustapha Klassou's lives.

They were a most unlikely couple, the Togolese Muslim businessman and the Saudi Arabian divorcee/refugee.

Even in the City of Ottawa, Ontario, where interracial couples from all walks of life could be seen at the mall, the local grocery store or on

College and University campuses, Mustapha and Zeinab definitely stood out. And they were more than okay with that.

"When you go to the appeal board, we should claim that we've been in a relationship for years, and use your old mail as proof of cohabitation, that way I can file for you," Mustapha proposed to Zeinab, a few months later.

Zeinab and Mustapha sat inside East Side Mario's restaurant at the Saint Laurent Mall, dining on tasty pierogis and sandwiches.

They'd taken the day off and were grabbing a bite before going to the movies at the Silver City theater in the east end.

The past six months had been absolutely wonderful for the two of them, and Zeinab thanked her angels in Jannah for the blessings that Mustapha brought to her life. Nevertheless, his words stunned her...

"Mustapha, my love, I cherish you but I cannot ask you that," Zeinab said hesitantly, and Mustapha smiled and took her hand, then brought it to his lips.

Zeinab looked at Mustapha, and licked her lips. Her heart thundered in her chest. Conflicting emotions stirred within her.

Truth be told, she'd fallen in love with this wonderful man, who treated her like a queen even though she had nothing.

As Zeinab walked around Ottawa with him, she was aware of the way people of other races gawked at Mustapha simply because he was a tall, dark-skinned African man.

Canadian society, for all of its supposed liberalism and multicultural policies, seemed very much against people of color, especially Black men.

Their racism irked her, and Zeinab always held Mustapha's hand with pride, in spite of the hateful glares that people, especially other Middle-Easterners, shot their way.

Haters gonna hate, Zeinab thought angrily. Staring back defiantly at those who held ill feelings for her and her lover, she garnered the strength to face them.

"Zeinab, I cherish you too, and I want to help you with this, not just because we're together but I've wanted to help you long before we got involved," Mustapha said earnestly.

Looking at him, Zeinab felt her face flush and her eyes grow moist. All the love that she felt for this amazing man poured forth and she grabbed Mustapha's face and kissed him.

When they came up for air, Zeinab looked at Mustapha adoringly. *Who am I to be loved this way ?* Zeinab thought, thankful to her lucky stars for such a find.

A couple of weeks later, Zeinab Al-Suwaiyel and Mustapha Klassou appeared before the Immigration & Refugee Board, and stated their case.

With help from Mustapha's cousin, attorney Ibrahim Klassou, they filed for Zeinab's permanent residence under the common law spouse clause.

The presiding Judge, a certain Latin American Judicial with liberal tendencies, granted them their fondest desire.

Amazed, Zeinab cried out in sheer joy, and then kissed Mustapha passionately. They thanked the

Judge profusely, and then exited the closed-door hearing, happy as can be.

"I've got more good news, my love," Zeinab said to Mustapha, as they rode the 95 bus from downtown Ottawa to Nepean, where they lived.

Mustapha sat next to her, with one arm around Zeinab's lovely shoulders while he texted with the other.

He was sharing news of their recent legal victory with friends and family members on Facebook when Zeinab took his hand, snatched away his cell phone, and pressed his hand gently against her belly.

"Oh my," Mustapha said, smiling nervously at Zeinab, and then excitement blossomed all over his face like flowers in the springtime.

113

Zeinab smiled and nodded firmly. A few days earlier, Zeinab had gone to her favorite clinic, and complained to her doctor of recent malaise she'd been experiencing.

Zeinab initially dismissed her discomfort as having to do with nervousness about her then-upcoming immigration hearing, until her doctor told her that she was pregnant.

Astonished by this surprising development, Zeinab nevertheless waited until after the hearing to share the news with her beloved Mustapha.

The young Saudi woman had been filled with dread as she and Mustapha went to the appeal board, and as it turns out, her worries were unfounded.

"From now on, you're going to be Baba Mustapha," Zeinab said, smiling at Mustapha, who grinned and kissed her hand.

"My love, you've made me so happy," Mustapha said excitedly and Zeinab rested her head on his shoulder, pleased by his reaction.

Everyone on the crowded OC Transpo bus looked at them, and the smiling couple happily ignored them. Indeed, they were very much in a world of their own.

As the bus reached Baseline Station, Zeinab and Mustapha got up and, in his excited state, Mustapha offered her a piggy back ride, which the tired Zeinab happily accepted.

"Let's get home quick, Baba, I'm hungry...and horny," Zeinab whispered into her man's ear, and Mustapha laughed.

115

Just like that, the happy couple began making their way home. Some drivers-by honked at them and waved.

Zeinab and Mustapha laughed at them and waved back. For the first time in forever, all is right with their world...

LET GO OF YOUR FEAR

"I am a Saudi Arabian Muslim woman who loves Black men, and I honestly don't apologize for it," Mariam Fahd said with a fearless smirk.

With that, Mariam looked at the big and tall, dark-skinned and ruggedly handsome young Zulu who stood before her.

Faisal Kwanele looked at her and gently shook his head. This Hijab-wearing Muslim gal from the Heartland of Islam was not what he was expecting, that's for damn sure.

What a woman, Faisal thought, as Mariam turned around, and he got a close look at her big round ass, which looked ready to burst from her yoga pants.

Leaning back on the couch, the international student from Johannesburg, South Africa, cast an appreciative glance at his lady love.

Faisal smiled at the curvaceous Muslim temptress who looked back at him fearlessly through lovely brown eyes. This was going to be a long night...

"Duly noted, beautiful, now come here," Faisal said, and a smiling Mariam went to him. Drawing her into his arms, Faisal kissed Mariam full and deep.

The young Saudi woman grinned as he gave her big round ass a firm slap. Mariam loved this more aggressive side of him.

Faisal was finally letting go of the shy guy routine and showing her what he was made of. Mariam found this positively thrilling...

From the moment Mariam Fahd first laid eyes on Faisal Kwanele during the International Students Orientation at Carleton University, the young Saudi Arabian Muslim woman decided to have him.

Six feet two inches tall, lean and athletic, with smooth chocolate skin and a shaved head, Faisal Kwanele was sexy the way only a proud son of Africa could be.

Upon moving to Ottawa, Ontario, from Dammam, Saudi Arabia, Mariam Fahd quickly noticed a big difference between Western men and men from other parts of the world.

A lot of guys in town went about swaggering, speaking loud and acting tough, but Faisal Kwanele was nothing like them.

The brother from Johannesburg carried himself with a natural confidence. Women could tell the difference, and Mariam Fahd was no exception...

That's why Mariam Fahd made sure of 'accidentally' bumping into Faisal Kwanele a number of times.

These run-ins occurred innocently of course, at various spots on campus, until the handsome Zulu got the hint and asked for her number.

That's how it all began. Mariam Fahd came to Carleton University in the City of Ottawa, Ontario, to study mechanical engineering...and also to have a good time.

With her conservative parents and siblings all the way in Dammam, Saudi Arabia, Mariam Fahd could finally do what she wanted.

With money in her pocket, thanks to a generous bursary from the Kingdom of Saudi Arabia's education ministry, Mariam Fahd lived like a queen in the City of Ottawa, Ontario.

The Saudi government paid for her tuition fees at Carleton University, and also room and board. On top of that, they also gave her a monthly stipend of seven hundred dollars. Not bad at all.

Considering that Mariam Fahd's school, rent, and groceries were already paid for, these extra seven hundred dollars were quite a bit of extra dough.

As long as Mariam didn't splurge too much, she could have a good time. Life was good to Mariam in the Canadian Capital.

At last, without the racist, sexist and xenophobic bozos from her culture to restrain her, the young Saudi Arabian Muslim woman got to explore her fondness for men of the African persuasion.

"What are you going to do to me ?" Mariam whispered, licking her lips as she sat on Faisal's lap.

Faisal caressed her breasts through her top, and looked into Mariam's eyes. Without another word, Faisal unzipped Mariam's top and freed her breasts from their flannel prison.

Gently Faisal caressed her areolas, and flicked his tongue on them. Mariam sighed happily, and urged Faisal to get on with it.

121

"I'm more into show than tell," Faisal finally replied, and he sat Mariam down on the couch, and went to work on her.

Off came her pants, and shoes, until only her panties remained. With a cocky grin, Faisal pulled down Mariam's purple panties, and looked at her sweet spot.

Like a lot of women from the Arab world, Mariam Fahd wasn't exactly a big believer in shaving down below.

This suited Faisal just fine because he wasn't about to turn down pussy because of a bit of hair. What man would ?

"Show me," Mariam said, and Faisal kissed her feet, and sucked on her toes, then began working his way up.

Spreading Mariam's thick thighs wide open, Faisal inhaled her unique womanly scent. As a smiling Mariam looked on, Faisal began eating her pussy.

The Zulu stud took his sweet time, teasing her clitoris with his tongue while his agile fingers slid into her wetness.

Mariam leaned back on the couch and spread her thighs wider, loving what Faisal was doing to her...

"Give me that ass, woman," Faisal said, and he put Mariam on all fours, and admired her thick round Saudi ass.

The women in Mariam's deeply religious and ultra-conservative homeland were known for their loveliness.

Not to mention the curves and big butts that they hid under their burkas haunted many a non-Saudi man's dream.

123

At last, Faisal got to see what the fuss is all about...and Mariam Fahd of Saudi Arabia definitely didn't disappoint.

"Do you like my thick Saudi ass, Mr. South Africa ?" Mariam teased, and Faisal grinned, then kissed her thick derriere.

Mariam purred with contentment as Faisal began fingering her wet pussy while licking her big tasty ass.

Spreading her thick ass cheeks wide open, Faisal began sliding his tongue up Mariam's warm, tight butthole.

Playfully smacking her ass, Faisal watched as Mariam made them cheeks jiggle, much to his delight.

"The things I'm going to do to that ass," Faisal said, much later, after polishing Mariam's tight butt hole with his tongue.

He was ready to fuck her but Mariam had other plans. Rising from the couch, Mariam knelt before Faisal and grabbed his dick, then began sucking it.

Faisal smiled as Mariam deep-throated his dick. Once the Saudi Arabian temptress had him good and hard, she got on all fours and shook her ass at him...

"Show me you're not all talk," Mariam said, licking her lips and winking at Faisal. The Zulu stud gripped her hips and rubbed his dick against her bum.

Mariam spread her thick ass cheeks wide open, exposing a fairly obvious target. Grinning, Faisal

125

grabbed some lotion and smeared it on her asshole, then pushed his dick inside.

A sharp groan escaped Mariam's lips as Faisal's dick popped into her asshole. Just like that, the Zulu stud began fucking her tight Saudi butt...

"Give me that ass," Faisal said, smacking Mariam's big round butt as he worked his dick up her asshole.

Face down and ass up, the young Saudi woman moaned deeply as Faisal's thick Zulu dick invaded her butt hole.

Grinding her fat ass against his groin, Mariam welcomed Faisal inside of her. With slow, deep strokes, Faisal filled Mariam's asshole and didn't let up until he came, much, much later.

The two lovebirds lay side by side on the carpeted floor, happy as can be. Until they began round two...

"To many more days like this one," Faisal Kwanele said, much later, as he lay in bed with Mariam lovingly wrapped up in his arms.

"Amen to that, handsome, handsome," Mariam replied, and they kissed once more before finally falling asleep.

MY SWEET PRINCE

Now I will show you all I've done for you my sweet Ali. Seriously, you think you're so damn tough and I'm supposedly soft and sweet.

When I smile at you while adjusting my Hijab or casually walking through the hallways of our University, I see you looking at me.

Lots of bronze-skinned, dark-eyed and raven-haired girls around but I am still one of a kind. I only pretend not to notice, but deep down inside, I absolutely love it.

Let's face it, girls dress up as much for other girls as we do the boys we adore. And Muslim sisters like myself are no exception.

"Amina where are you going ?", someone hollers, and my heart skips a beat. I freeze in front of the elevator as I hear your voice. I turn around and smile nonchalantly.

"I'm off to class Ali," I shrug, looking you up and down. I love looking into your eyes, my handsome face.

128

My eyes flit from your rugged, handsome face, to your broad shoulders, well-defined chest, and overall lean, athletic physique camouflaged by your baggy clothes.

That chocolate glistens in the early afternoon sunlight, adding to your already considerable charms.

"You're always in a rush", you say, smiling at me. Ah, my sweet, ever-clueless Ali. With your blue T-shirt and White sweatpants, you've got Somali written all over you.

Guys from your part of the world are my weakness but you'll never get me to actually admit it.

"Some of us actually want to graduate and get out of Carleton", I say icily, and you briefly pout, though it's fleeting.

129

"Alright mama," you say casually, shrugging as if nothing ever gets to you. Such an Ali thing to do in the face of opposition. You're simply imperturbable and nothing can pierce your shell.

Not the stares you endure as you walk through the halls of our school or on the streets of Ottawa, nothing on this earth.

You've got your game face on, the Black man's legendary bravado. "Are you coming to the Islamic Scholars Association Banquet?" I ask innocently, my eyes boring into yours.

"Nobody told me about it, when is it?" You say, hope all too evident on your face. Your eyes stare into mine with a disarming mixture of eagerness and innocence.

Groaning in mock frustration, I casually pull out a flyer from my purse and hand it to you.

130

"It's next Saturday at the NAC," I say, practically shoving the flyer into your hands. You read the flyer, and your handsome face lights up like a Christmas tree, for lack of a better term.

"Thank you so much Amina," you say quite enthusiastically, squeezing me into a passionate bear hug.

I pretend to be bothered but deep down, I totally love it. "You're welcome Ali, I hope to see you there."

The elevator doors swing open at last, and we rush inside. Two other students join us, a large Hindu guy and a blonde-haired White gal in a short skirt.

Her lack of modesty irks my Saudi sensibilities but I flash her a polite smile.

131

The tart has the nerve to scratch her voluminous derriere, while standing right in front of us, and I notice your eyes zero in on her.

"Ouch," you yelp as I accidentally step on your foot. My high heels 'accidentally' dig into your soft sneakers.

"I'm sorry," I say with all the sincerity of a desert fox eyeing a vulnerable rabbit. You smile at me.

The elevators in the University center aren't the best but at last, we arrive on the fourth floor. We exit. You stand there, looking at me with an odd look on your face.

"Thanks for giving me this, mamas," you say, and the gratitude in your voice warms my heart. I smile up at you, and step forward, barely containing the urge to embrace you.

And then you drive a stake through my heart. " I wonder who I'm going to go with," you say, grinning, before rubbing my head in a patronizing manner.

I am seething inside. "See you later sister," you say, then trot off to your next class. I watch as you dash through the throngs of students in the Atrium, and make your way to the Tory building.

"Damn you Ali," I fume, all the while admiring your cute butt as you run. Damn you to the depths of hell.

With a deep, profound sigh, I make my way to my first class of the day. Sociology of

Deviance is a tough course, but it's a required one for all Law and Criminology majors.

The professor is a tough cookie but I attended the prestigious and all-female Dar Al-Hanan School in my native Jeddah, Saudi Arabia. I think I can handle what Canadian University academics throw at me.

At least they don't believe in corporal punishment as a form of discipline for pupils here. Such a damn shame.

"What's up Miss Al-Gosaibi ?" comes a loud female voice, snapping me out of my interesting reverie.

I look to my right and notice my friend and roommate Deborah Rosenthal, a plump, red-haired and green-eyed gal in tight dark clothing, what they call Goth chic in the West.

134

"Hi Deb," I say with all the enthusiasm of a woman marching to death row. Deb and I met during Orientation Day at Carleton two years ago.

We were both newcomers to Canada, and international students to boot. Deborah is originally from Berkshire, England, and get a load of this, she's Jewish.

Now, you wouldn't think that I, Amina Al-Gosaibi, the daughter of a powerful Saudi Arabian sheikh, and a proud Muslim woman, would be friends with a Jewish chick from Britain, and you'd be dead wrong.

Allah puts certain people in our path so we can learn from them. Deb is one of my best friends.

"You look like you got the blues," Deb chides me as she elbows me in the ribs none too gently. We're walking through the quad on our way to the Loeb building.

"Don't want to talk about it," I say meekly, trying to get the image of one Ali Waberi, Ottawa-born Somali civil engineering student, Carleton University skirt chaser and wannabe rapper out of my head.

Deb isn't letting me off the hook that easily. "You saw Ali again," Deb laughs, and I shoot her a warning glare.

Seriously, why does she have to go there ? "Invite me to the wedding," Deb laughs as we enter our class.

I head to my seat in the middle of the second row, and Deb joins me. "If you like a guy you have to find a way to let him know," she whispers.

I roll my eyes. "I invited him to the NAC event and was about to tell him I had an extra ticket but he didn't let me finish," I say softly. The thought of seeing Ali with another gal irks me.

"Got to let the fellas know when we like them because they're not good at reading hints," Deb laughs, and I smile.

Her mirth is decidedly contagious. I've been living in Ottawa, Ontario, for a couple of years now.

My parents, Khan and Manal Al-Gosaibi, still live back in Jeddah with my younger brothers Alharbi and Yousef and I miss them dearly. I usually go home in the summer. Not this past summer.

I stayed in Ottawa, got a work permit and actually got myself a job. I worked at Wal-Mart, where I met a tall, cute young Somali guy named Ali Waberi.

Life hasn't been the same for me since. I think I'm falling in love with him. The guy is clueless, and he flirts with everything on two legs.

My heart thunders in my breast every time Ali looks at me. Allah help me. I can't help the way I feel.

"I'm sure you'll get your chocolate prince charming in the end, " Deb teases, and I hiss. I'm about to swat her upside the head when the Prof walks in.

138

"Fun time is over," I groan, and Deb nods. Class breezes by, and then I rush out. It's noon and I'm famished.

"Later Mina," Deb says, and then she's off to her next class. I go to a nearby prayer room, pray for a few minutes, then exit.

I make my way to the University center, and into the food court. At this hour, the place is packed with people.

I walk to my favorite spot, and buy some Chinese food. Shrimp-fried rice with veggies, and sit down. Solo.

In a vast cafeteria filled with students of all races and nationalities, I am sitting alone. My hunger gnaws at me even as I eat, and I realize that what I hunger for isn't food.

At the table nearest mine, a young couple is making out. A tall, spiky-haired White guy with tattoos and piercings is kissing a dark-skinned young woman with dreadlocks. Probably Jamaican by the looks of her.

In spite of their lack of modesty, I gaze upon them with envy rather than disgust. "You're so lucky," I mutter to myself, gazing at the dark-skinned female as she kisses her boyfriend.

I realize that I'm staring and promptly return my gaze to my food. I continue looking around the cafeteria.

A couple of plump White girls walk by, hand in hand. A young Hindu guy kisses a Chinese gal's hand and she giggles while looking at him adoringly. Why can't I have what they have ?

In my religion and culture, we have many restrictions as far as interactions between unmarried men and women. Such is our society.

In Saudi Arabia, the strictest of Muslim countries, much of what ordinary men and women consider normal behavior would get you arrested by the Mutaween or Saudi vice police. I envy Westerners sometimes, I truly do.

"Boo !" a loud male voice shouts, inches from my ear, snapping me out of my musings. I whirl around, shocked. Ali's smirking face is inches from mine.

My heart skips a beat. "You bastard," I say, shaking my head and clutching my chest with one hand. "I got you good," Ali laughs, looking me up and down.

I roll my eyes, refusing to admit it. Seriously, the last thing I want to do is give him a bigger head.

"Got a minute?" Ali asks, pulling up a chair and sitting across from me. Feigning annoyance, I look him up and down.

"Make yourself at home," I say with a shrug. I look at Ali, and the seriousness on his dark, handsome face surprises me.

He's the eternal joker, the guy who pranks men and women regardless of whether he's at work or at school. "I got something to discuss with you," he says.

"Need help with your elective homework again I take it," I smirk and nod with a touch of sheer condescendence.

Like most students in majors such as mathematics, engineering or science, Ali can't make heads or tails of humanities-type stuff like sociology, psychology or law.

It doesn't compute with their geek brains, I guess. "Nah I'm cool," Ali says. Last semester, I practically did all of his homework for him when he took psychology as an elective.

I griped while doing it but I was happy to help Ali. Anything to get closer to the big lug. I need him.

Ali shakes his head and looks at me. Gently, he lays his big hand on mine. "Amina, I think I like you," Ali says, shrugging, his eyes staring intensely into mine.

My heart skips a beat. Cold sweat rushes between my shoulder blades. "I see," I say evenly.

Though outwardly calm, inside I'm elated. I feel like jumping for joy. Ali likes me. Ali likes me !

"This a ploy to get a free ticket to the NAC from me ?" I ask casually, in my usual snarky tone.

Ali groans in frustration. "I knew this was a mistake," he says, shaking his head. He rises to leave.

I grab his hand with all the force I can muster. I'm only five-foot-four and quite slim, I look tiny next to a tall, athletic guy like Ali.

But I am strong when I need to be. Always have been. And I may have made the mistake of a lifetime by pushing Ali too far.

How could I have been so foolish? The guy just bared his heart to me and I was so snide and cold to him. Too chicken to admit the feelings I've had for him for the longest time.

"What are you doing?" Ali asks, looking at my tiny hand gripping his wrist like a vise. I take a deep breath and look into his eyes.

"This," I say, and grab him by the collar of his sky-blue T-shirt. Then I kissed him.

That's right, I stood on my tippy toes, grabbed Ali, the macho Somali who acts like he owns Carleton, and I kissed him.

In front of everybody. In the University center food court. How do you like them apples ?

"Whoa," Ali said, looking at me uncertainly when we came up for air. I am honestly pleased by his reaction.

"In case that was unclear for your male brain I like you too Ali," I smile. Ali grins, and sits back down. I entwined my hands in his.

"You've got sweet lips Miss Saudi Arabia," Ali grins. I wink at him. "Amen to that," I smile happily.

Everyone is staring at us, but I don't care. Not every day you see a pious, Hijab-wearing Muslim sister, from Saudi Arabia of all places, kissing a Black man, out in the open.

146

If I were in my country, my actions would be considered criminal. Women and men who engage in relations outside of marriage, even if they're both single, are harshly punished in Saudi Arabia.

Death is the punishment for adultery. If my parents knew about my feelings for Ali, they'd be horrified and our whole family would be scandalized.

My life might have been in jeopardy. However, I'm in Ontario, Canada. Literally thousands upon thousands of miles from the Kingdom of Saudi Arabia.

I'm with Ali, and he's with me. Let people think what they will. *I honestly don't care. I do my own thing.*

147

"Let's take a walk mamas," Ali says, and I clasp my hand in his proudly as we make our way out of the University center food court and down the stairs.

"I'm happy you told me today because I've had feelings for you since last summer," I confessed to Ali, who laughs.

Ali gently strokes my face. I kiss his fingers when they brush against my lips. He is so beautiful and so sweet, so good to me just like I always knew he would.

"And you never said anything, Ali says, shaking his head. I shrug. I don't know how I feel about that.

"Hesitation will always be my fatal flaw, but I am ready to start living," I said evenly. Ali pulls me into his arms and kisses me.
148

"Good answer mamas," Ali laughs. Thus we took our first stroll together as an actual couple. Just two people enjoying each other's company.

Tonight, when I go home, I'm going to have so much to tell Deb, about this wonderful new development.

Ali told me he liked me, and I kissed Ali, right in front of everybody ! So much for the stereotype about Saudi Arabian women being meek, eh ?

For now, though, I'm walking tall, hand in hand with the one I cherish above all others. Don't know where this all leads but for now, I'm one happy woman.

A life is passion, that's what I aspire for. I've wasted too much time living in the shadows, afraid to take chances.

149

The way I see it, it's never too late to make up for lost time. I embrace the ways of passion and don't look back.

Wish me luck. I have a good feeling about this one, for sure. We're going to be just fine. Insha'Allah.

SOME SAUDI WOMEN ARE BOSSY

You are one crazy broad, I thought to myself as I woke up, all cuffed up, after one helluva night, in my girlfriend Mariam Alzahrani's bed.

Man, I went to *Mansion Night Club* the night before for an *African Student Union* party, and I barely remember anything.

Not exactly standard fare for yours truly, I must insist on saying. My name is Kader Suleiman and I'm a young Black man of Somali descent living in the City of Ottawa, Ontario.

Typically, I'm not the type to go to clubs because, to be honest, that's not really my type of scene.

I'm just a Somali brother from the City of Calgary, Alberta, living in Ottawa while studying business administration at Carleton University.

Prior to moving to Ontario for school, I'd never even left provincial Alberta, where I was born and raised.

My parents, Yousef and Hodan Suleiman moved to Alberta from their ancestral hometown of Boorame, southWestern Somalia, in the 1980s.

"Mariam, are you going to untie me or what ?"
I asked, sighing, as I looked at my tightly bound
hands and feet.

I'm kinky and quite open-minded, don't get me
wrong, but the linchpin of all things BDSM is
supposed to be consent.

Otherwise it'll be the Jian Ghomeshi affair all
over again, only the male version. I looked at
Mariam, who stood at the foot of the bed,
smirking.

"You forgot to say please lover boy," Mariam
said, wagging her little finger at me. I looked
at her, temporarily distracted by how sexy
Mariam looked in a blue T-shirt and Black thong,
and shook my head.

I willed myself to be calm, not an easy thing to do considering the rude awakening I've just had.

From the moment I first laid eyes on Mariam, I knew that this broad was trouble. Still, since I was thinking with my dick at the time, I went after her with everything I've got.

Look, I've got a thing for Arab girls, alright ? A lot of Somali brothers do, but they won't admit it.

Me ? I find Arab girls simply irresistible. Lots of Arab guys marry Somali women, but you rarely see a Somali guy with an Arab chick.

Sounds like a serious imbalance and a bit of a double standard to me, so I set out to rectify the situation as best I can.

153

Ever since high school, I've only dated Arab girls. When I went to the Senior Prom at Laurier Academy in Calgary's South End, I went with eighteen-year-old Stephanie Aoun, a lovely Lebanese Christian cutie I met in my math class.

You should have seen the way the Arab guys at school looked at us as we happily danced together.

A tall Somali brother in a tuxedo and a short, cute Arab chick in a bright red evening gown. Stephanie and I made a cute couple.

That night, we made love for the first time. Having gotten a taste of Arab booty at eighteen, I became addicted.

Now that I'm in University, I see no reason to change my dating habits. Hence why I'm with Mariam here.

154

The tall, voluptuous Saudi Arabian cutie with the dark bronze skin, curly Black hair and simply mesmerizing golden brown eyes took my breath away.

Even clad in a pullover sweater, traditional long skirt and Hijab, Mariam Alzahrani moved with a sensual grace that was almost hypnotic.

I watched her sashaying that thick Arab booty of hers from side to side like a pendulum of temptation in the Atrium at Carleton, and swore to myself that this woman would be mine.

"You gave me quite a scare last night," Mariam said, her loud voice snapping me out of my little reverie.

I looked at her, and some concern on her pretty face instead of the usual devil-may-care grin I'm accustomed to seeing.

155

Mariam and I have a complicated relationship, to say the least. At times it's a volatile relationship.

Whoever thinks Saudi Arabian women are polite, soft and sweet has obviously never met her. Mariam is one BOSSY broad, in every way.

"I'm sorry about that babe," I said in a soft, caring tone while looking directly into Mariam's eyes.

Every woman loves to hear "I'm sorry" for her guy, I learned this early on. I willed my face to mimic pure sincerity, and prayed that Mariam wasn't feeling cynical today.

We usually have fun, her and I. Hell, Mariam is the who introduced me to bondage and all that kinky shit. Makes for a fun sexual experience, let me tell you.

156

"Nice try, Kader, but you're not getting out of these cuffs until we've had a serious talk," Mariam said, laughing.

I smiled sweetly, and seriously wished I could wring her pretty little neck. Hmmm. No, I don't seriously want to her but this bitch is getting on my last fucking nerve. Great, now Mariam wants to get her speech on and I've got to pee.

"I'm all ears," I said with a smile, wondering how in hell I always end up in situations like this.

Last year, I hooked up with this Syrian Christian broad named Mara Alkhani in Edmonton, Alberta, and her Muslim husband Samir caught us in bed together.

The dude actually came after me with a machete. I'm lucky I got out of there in one piece.

Luckily Mara called the cops, and they came along right away. The Edmonton police servicemen who responded to Mara's frantic 911 call arrived on the scene just as Samir was about to chop my head off in the Alkhani household's driveway.

The fucker was actually going to kill me ! They shot the crazy mofo, but he survived. Samir swore revenge upon me, though.

That's part of the reason why I moved to Ottawa for University. I'm a wanted man in Alberta, in more ways than one.

"Last night, you got into it with Abdul and if not for me your ass would be dead or in jail,"

Mariam said, crossing her arms over her spectacular chest.

A gesture I found distracting, for my sweetie is definitely a busty gal. I nodded, vaguely remembering some Qatari dude getting in my face at the club, before the bouncers got involved.

I had a lot of beer in me, Alexander Keith's from Nova Scotia, and as you may well know, we Somalis don't handle our liquor too well.

"I'm sorry about that babe, I should have been less of a hothead," I said, allowing my eyes to droop a bit.

Truth be told, it was out of tiredness rather than shame. Who cares, though ? With females, you've got to tell them what they want to hear.

I licked my lips, and realized that my lower lip was fatter than usual. Was it because of Abdul's fist connecting with my jaw?

"When I saw Abdul and his friends come after you I just lost it," Mariam said, and I saw her dark eyes go moist.

When I saw that, and realized that her concern was genuine, my heart wrenched in my chest. I don't usually deal with females who actually give a damn about me.

I'm a young brother in Canada who dates foreign females. To them, I'm fun, edgy, and great entertainment, in and out of bed, but not usually someone worth an emotional investment.

"I've been such a fool," I said, no longer acting. I reached for Mariam, wishing to embrace my sweetie and assure her of my sincerity, but

160

with my hands and feet bound to the bed, I couldn't very well get at her.

Mariam looked at me, and her lips trembled. Lips that kissed me passionately more times than I could count, and brought me enormous pleasure. I wanted to kiss Mariam and hold her and never let go.

"You're such a fool," Mariam said, smiling faintly and shaking her head. I watched as she came to me, and hugged me tight.

I hugged her back, as much as my bound hands would allow. Mariam took my face in her hands, and looked into my eyes.

I smiled sheepishly, wishing I could convey to her how badly I felt. I don't feel bad about decking Abdul, not one bit.

I knew that if I got into it with that bozo, he definitely had it coming. No, I felt bad for worrying Mariam, my sweetheart.

I've certainly never met someone like Mariam, that's for damn sure. This gal has a fairly interesting background.

Born in the City of Dammam, eastern Saudi Arabia, and raised in the City of Toronto, Ontario, this feisty, curvaceous and outspoken gal is definitely a handful but I honestly can't get enough of her.

Like me, Mariam comes from a staunchly conservative Muslim family. Like me, she moved to Ottawa to get away from her folks and live la vida loca.

We're quite a pair, her and I. What can I say ?
I got a thing for bossy Arab ladies, especially
Hijabis. Don't Judge me, I just can't help myself.

"What would I do without you ?" I said to
Mariam, with my face inches from hers. Mariam
smiled, and shrugged.

Pulling her close, I kissed her again. Mariam
pressed her sinfully sexy curves against me, and
desire rose in me, sharp and demanding.

There's something about the way a woman
smells in the morning that always frigging turns
me on.

Seriously, before females put on all the perfumes
and all that glop supposedly to impress guys or
other females, they forget their own natural
scent.

For me, there's nothing more erotic. I reached for Mariam's breasts, and felt them through the faded old blue T-shirt she had on.

"Yummy," I said with a wry grin, and Mariam sighed happily as I reached under her shirt and began gently massaging her boobies.

Now, like ninety nine point nine percent of all Black man, I am an ass man but to me, boobies aren't a distant second when it comes to favorite places in a woman's body.

Yup, I love them big butts on brown women but I always notice a busty gal. Always. Mariam pulled her T-shirt off, exposing her boobs, and I happily sucked on one while caressing the other.

"Go for it habibi," Mariam whispered, and I did as I was told, not that I needed any frigging encouragement, mind you.

I sucked on my sweetie's succulent breasts, and then licked a path from her boobs to her belly.

As I licked a path toward her pelvic region, I sensed some hesitation on Mariam's part. I looked up at her, and saw anxiety on her lovely face.

"I haven't showered yet," Mariam said, biting her lip. Dammit, why are females so self-conscious at times ?

I swear, each woman is the harshest Judge of herself. I looked at Mariam, and shook my head.

Certain times, a woman's insecurities can be quite taxing to us men, but I willed myself to be calm and searched for the right thing to say.

"Mariam, my angel, I love the way you smell and taste," I said, smiling, and the look of surprise I saw on her beautiful face thrilled me.

Mariam bit her lip, and then, spread her thighs invitingly. Yes, I thought victoriously, and pulled down her Black thong.

Mariam's hairy bush stared at me. I buried my face between her legs, inhaling her womanly scent. Happily, I went to work on her.

"Hmmm just like that," Mariam said, sighing deeply as I licked her pussy thoroughly, sliding my fingers in there and alternately teasing, licking and tasting her sweet spot.

My Saudi Arabian goddess lay on the bed, writhing and moaning as I worked my magic on her.

I love them sounds Mariam made. Tells me I'm on the right track. Unless she's faking, that is, I thought darkly. Hey, females do that, alright?

Much later, after I coaxed at least one loud, wet orgasm out of her, it was Mariam's turn to pleasure yours truly.

I leaned back and relaxed, my head comfortably resting on the pillows, as Mariam held my dick with both hands and sucked on it.

Man, it doesn't get any better than this. That's exactly how every man should start the day, wouldn't you say?

"Love the way you taste Kader," Mariam said, in mid-suck, and I smiled before gently rubbing her head, my way of reminding her to focus on the task at hand.

167

I was already hard as a piston, and Mariam pumped her hand up and down my shaft while sucking on my dick head like a frigging lollipop. I frigging love it when she does that. The lady definitely knows what I like.

Mariam polished my fuck stick, and then, we got down to business. First Mariam straddled me.

The young woman shrieked while impaling herself on my dick and rode me hard while I held her by the hips and slammed my dick into her cunt.

Doing her like this was alright, but I didn't really, really start enjoying myself until we did it doggy style.

I put Mariam on all fours, gave her thick Saudi booty a kiss, and massaged it a bit before easing my dick into her from behind.

"Give it to me hard," Mariam said, as if I needed any encouragement. I put my hands on those wide hips of hers and sighed happily as I beheld her thick booty, which swallowed my dick.

I thrust into her, loving the feel of her tight cunt gripping my dick like a vise. Mariam has one of the most amazing asses I've ever seen.

I once asked her to try anal sex but, um, our experiment into backdoor loving ended up messily.

Since then, I've stuck to what I know. And what I know is banging the pussy RIGHT, and that's exactly what I did to Mariam.

I buried my dick in her cunt, and smacked that big ass of hers. I can't get enough of her thick booty.

My sweetie squealed in delight as I pounded her, and we fucked and sucked the morning away. Seriously, it was almost noon by the time we stopped.

"That was fun," I said to Mariam, as we lay side by side on her bed, which reeked of our smells and juices.

Mariam nodded, and kissed me gently. I tasted myself on her lips, and smiled wickedly at the realization. I didn't tell her THAT, though.

Got to be tactful at times, you know ? I looked at my sweetie, and gently caressed her long, lustrous Black hair.

"You're going to unbind me or what ?" I asked, and a laughing Mariam pretended to hesitate before reaching for the keys.

I thought about asking her where in hell she got the cuffs, but realized the futility of such a question.

Mariam is a freaky mama who loves all things BDSM. Hell, one time, while sucking me off, Mariam shoved a butt plug in my ass.

Look, it was a fun experience and got me real hard but I don't get down like that. I told Mariam we wouldn't be trying that stuff again anytime soon.

"Spend the day with me, I'll make us dinner," Mariam said, after freeing me. I rubbed my hands, and nodded.

I watched as Mariam put her clothes back on, and the way her big Saudi butt swallowed that lacy Black thong caused me to feel a stir down below.

Sorry, I'm an ass man, as I said before. Mariam bent down to pick up something, and I got hard again.

"Make the bed while I go make lunch, habib, oh, and here's your cell phone," Mariam said, as she tossed me my precious Blackberry.

I barely caught it, and shot Mariam a look. Seriously, I love her but I don't like it when anyone messes with my electronics.

Luckily I've got insurance on the damn thing, and it's password protected. I trust Mariam, of course, but a man's got to have his privacy.

I smiled at Mariam and waved at her as she left the room, and then my smile vanished when I saw that someone had changed the wallpaper on my phone's screen.

The previous wallpaper showed my favorite *Samuel L. Jackson* meme from Facebook, the one where he says "May the force be with you motherfucker".

The new wallpaper showed Mariam and I holding hands at the Saint Laurent Mall, our favorite hangout.

"Bitch found out my password," I said to myself, amazed. I thought about confronting her, but fuck it, I decided not to.

I've had one helluva night, but my morning started out on a good note. Why ruin things? I sat on the bed, relaxing a bit.

173

Mariam definitely wore me out today, man. Kinky, bossy and unpredictable, all the things I absolutely love about my lady.

"Kader, go shower already, fool, dinner's almost ready," Mariam's voice shrieked from the kitchen, setting me on edge.

The nerve on that woman, I thought, as I bit back a reply. Rolling my eyes, I headed to the washroom.

I felt filthy, to tell you the truth, but in a good way. Sex has a unique aroma and one that I find quite pleasant.

As I passed the kitchen on my way there, I saw Mariam, a vision of beauty, singing while cooking in the kitchen.

174

I smelled some tasty *Al Kabsa*, a traditional meal of rice and chicken that's popular in Saudi Arabia.

I laughed to myself, and thankfully Mariam didn't hear me because she had her headphones on.

While cooking and singing, Mariam was shaking that ass of hers. *What a woman*, I thought, and stepped into the shower.

I thought of all the fun and wicked things that Mariam and I did together. The fun is just beginning, trust me.

Yup, my bossy sweetie Mariam is definitely a handful but I wouldn't have my kinky Saudi Arabian Muslim sweetheart any other way.

As I began to clean myself up, lathering myself with water and soap, I visualized Mariam's ass, and grinned as I began stroking my hard dick.

WHEN YOU OPEN YOURSELF UP

"I just don't get you, Mohammed, I know for a fact that you hate me, you bad-mouth me in front of Walmart associates, you even complain about me through official channels, and now, you want to tell me that you have feelings for me ? Fuck you, you two-faced asshole," Maimuna Ali said vehemently.

With that, the slender young Saudi-Canadian Muslim woman angrily repressed a shudder as she gazed upon one Mohammed Adewale. The absolute frigging nerve on that dude !

176

Glaring angrily at the big and tall young Nigerian Muslim man who stood before her, Maimuna Ali bit down the urge to smack the fool.

Moving from her hometown of Jeddah, Saudi Arabia, a few years back proved to be hard as hell for Maimuna Ali, but she adjusted to life in the Canadian Capital.

Maimuna came to the City of Ottawa, Ontario, to make a fresh start after the end of her marriage to Youssef Obeid.

While studying at University, Maimuna got herself a job as a customer service manager at the local Walmart.

Most people assumed the job of a C.S.M. was boring, but the drama that Maimuna Ali had to endure begged to differ.

Case in point ? Her rather complex relationship with Mohammed the taciturn security guard, for example.

After talking shit about Maimuna for ages, Mohammed Adewale had the temerity to ask her for a parlay at McDonald's on his day off.

Reluctantly Maimuna showed up, wondering what her erstwhile nemesis had in mind. The bozo ended up surprising the hell out of her with his revelations...

"Look, Maimuna, I'm sorry about that, it's just that, well, recently, I made a surprising discovery about myself," Mohammed said, and he looked at Maimuna in a way he never had before.

Maimuna had been working as a customer service manager at the Walmart for the past four years, and as a problem solver, it fell to her to get associates, and others, to get the job done.

Managing people didn't come easy, and as the one to make the tough decisions, Maimuna Ali was far from one of the most popular people in the store.

"What did you discover about yourself?" Maimuna asked tersely, curious in spite of herself. When Mohammed first started working as a security guard for the store, they got along famously.

They were both students at Canada's Capital University, working at the store to make a few bucks. They even started to become friends. And then things started to go wrong.

Before long, Maimuna was snapping at Mohammed for taking too long on his breaks, and he was calling her a cold and heartless bitch behind her back. How did they get here?

179

"I'm attracted to bossy women, especially bossy Arab women, I'm submissive," Mohammed said evenly, and Maimuna's eyes went wide.

If she'd been struck by lightning inside the McDonald's restaurant located inside one of Ottawa's busiest Walmart stores, Maimuna wouldn't have been more shocked.

Mohammed always carried himself like he owned the place, fearlessly dealing with angry clients while chatting with his female admirers, among them several of Maimuna's co-workers. She was not expecting that...

"What the fuck ?" Maimuna blurted out, and she looked at Mohammed as though he had two poisonous heads.

For the past few months he'd been telling everyone how he thought she was mean and bossy, his

180

sworn enemy and a poor excuse for a human being.

Like a lot of Muslim brothers, Mohammed simply did not like to see a young Arab woman in charge. Or so she thought.

Mohammed's latest revelation had Maimuna's head spinning, and with good reason. It completely changed the way she thought about him...

"Well, um, Maimuna, when you're bossing me around and shit, I like it, a lot, but I don't like the fact that I like it," Mohammed said, exhaling sharply, and he fixed his gaze on Maimuna.

The young woman leaned back in her chair, absolutely astonished by what she'd just heard. She looked at Mohammed, unaware of what to say. Seriously, how does a woman respond to such a statement ?

181

"Mohammed, if you like me, why do you hate me and bad-mouth me ?" Maimuna said, sighing deeply. Mohammed looked at her and smiled faintly, and then he gently brushed his hand against hers.

Maimuna looked at his hand on hers and hesitated, but did not pull back. Looking at Mohammed expectantly, she awaited the big man's answer. This ought to be good, Maimuna thought indignantly.

"When I see you, I want to get on my damn knees and worship you, my strong and dominant Muslim goddess, but I am also ashamed to feel this way because I was raised to be a strong Black Muslim man," Mohammed confessed, and Maimuna could have sworn she saw his eyes grow moist.

Maimuna understood that something terribly sensitive was happening inside Mohammed's mind

182

and soul, but she couldn't resist chastising him a bit...

"Well, bozo, that's too bad, instead of admitting to yourself what you want, in your pathetic confusion, you almost cost me everything, I should go to the manager about what you just told me and get your ass fired," Maimuna said snidely, and instead of flinching and pleading like she expected him to,

Mohammed Adewale looked almost relieved. Now it was her turn to be puzzled and contrite. The brother's behavior was confusing Maimuna a whole damn lot...

"It's true, Maimuna, it's what I deserve, I am attracted to your strength and your beauty but I wasn't man enough to tell you from the jump that I like, no, love your bossy ways, I understand if you want me gone," Mohammed said, and then the big guy stood up, bowed his head gently and then turned to leave.

Maimuna looked Mohammed up and down, noticed how cute his ass looked in a blue silk shirt and Black silk pants, and smiled. A wicked idea sprang into her conniving mind...

"Mohammed, come back here and sit your ass back down, dammit, I did not give you permission to leave," Maimuna said in a sharp, bossy tone, and Mohammed turned around, smiled faintly and did as he was told.

I can work with this one, Maimuna thought to herself, and she made a show of wringing her fingers.

Mohammed would be a wonderful toy for a natural sadist like her to play with, if he could follow instruction, of course. The question is, how far was he willing to go ?

"What does mademoiselle Maimuna expect of me ?" Mohammed asked hopefully, and Maimuna grinned broadly.

This was going to be lots of fun, she could feel it. Looking at Mohammed, feelings that Maimuna long thought buried and gone resurfaced.

Maimuna felt a tingle between her legs. She'd long fancied the big man, and the prospect of getting her hands on him appealed to her immensely.

"Mohammed, if you agree to let me be your Mistress, you will become mine, I will own you and make your life sweet life, and in submitting to me, your strong Muslim goddess, you will know fulfillment," Maimuna said evenly, and Mohammed stroked his goateed chin thoughtfully.

185

Maimuna could almost see the wheels turning in his mind. And she had a fair idea what he was thinking...

In her time, Maimuna Ali had been called a lot of things. A cruel, sadistic bitch. A mean-spirited control freak. A psychotic cunt with anger issues. A passive aggressive evil bitch. And so much more.

Truth be told, she was far simpler than that. Control is all that Maimuna desires. Control over others, for their own good, of course.

While living in Ottawa, Maimuna discovered the world of BDSM and the dearth of Muslim women in it.

A rather unfortunate situation which the young Saudi Arabian woman set out to rectify as the first Muslim dominatrix...

The benevolent dictator in female form, that's the true essence of the lovely, feisty lady known as Maimuna Ali in a nutshell.

Indeed, Maimuna Ali wears a lot of different hats. University student, BDSM expert, customer service manager at Walmart, and yet, she's still that pious, Hijab-wearing Muslim sister you see at the Masjid on Fridays.

Looking at Mohammed Adewale, Maimuna Ali awaited his response. Of course, like all Muslim men, he feared Muslim female strength and would run and hide.

Resigned to being rejected yet again by another Muslim male submissive who was afraid of what she represented, Maimuna sighed and sipped on her Pepsi.

Mohammed hesitated and Maimuna braced herself for the inevitable, upcoming rejection. Story of her life.

Being a dominant Muslim woman meant being feared and hated by the ones she loved the most, the Muslim men of the world...

"Mistress Maimuna, I pledge myself to you," Mohammed Adewale said without hesitation or shame, and then inside the crowded McDonald's restaurant, something amazing happened.

The tall, strong-looking and well-dressed brother genuflected before the slender young Arab woman and gallantly took her sleek hand in his before kissing it.

Maimuna blushed, astonished by what Mohammed had just done...and she was quite pleased by the unexpected gesture.

"You are mine," Maimuna whispered breathlessly, and Mohammed smiled. Throwing herself into his massive arms, Maimuna kissed Mohammed passionately.

Thus, the two of them reconciled. Store employers and shoppers alike gaped in astonishment as the two of them walked out of Walmart, hand in hand.

They needn't have been surprised. Lots of Muslim men secretly love bossy Muslim women. It simply takes a strong brother to admit it...

"Oh yes," Mohammed said, smiling as he stood against the wall of Maimuna's basement, his arms and legs tied.

Maimuna stood before him, clad in a Black tank top and Black leather miniskirt, sans panties, her dark bronze skin glistening in the low lit room.

In her right hand, Maimuna held a whip, and with the left, she lovingly stroked an object of a decidedly phallic nature.

A shiny silvery strap-on dildo which Maimuna bought just for her new sub. Putting it back in her purse, Maimuna looked at Mohammed and licked her lips...

"Hmm, this is going to be so much fun," Maimuna said, smiling, and then she scowled and glared at Mohammed, slipping into dominatrix mode.

Walking up to Mohammed, she grabbed his dark, handsome face. Looking into Mohammed's eyes, Mistress Maimuna saw both lust and fear.

Slapping him hard across the face, Mistress Maimuna watched as the big Black man flinched, and then smiled.

190

"Nice, thank you Mistress Maimuna," Mohammed said, and the young Arab woman grinned upon hearing that.

Grabbing Mohammed's dick and balls, Mistress Maimuna squeezed them none too gently, and Mohammed cried out.

Next, she let go of his junk and made Mohammed turn around, not an easy thing considering he was chained up.

Donning gloves, Mistress Maimuna proceeded to spank Mohammed's ass, loving the way the big man's cheeks jiggled.

"Mohammed, I love you, and I hate you, and I'm going to make your life sweet hell," Mistress Maimuna said, laughing.

Mohammed gulped, and Maimuna saw fear, actual fear, on his face and drank it in. Nothing she loved

191

more than forcing men to face their fear of female power...

Grabbing Mohammed's belt, she proceeded to whoop his ass with it, and he whimpered as she gave him a well-deserved thrashing.

Mistress Maimuna smiled, pleased with herself as she whipped Mohammed's bum. The way she figured it, if more Muslim women spanked Black Muslim men, the world would be a better place...

"Hmm, that was fun," Mohammed said, sighing happily, and Mistress Maimuna undid his restraints, and then led him around the house on a leash and chain.

As Mohammed followed Mistress Maimuna on all fours, he admired her nice ass and how awesome it looked in her Black leather miniskirt.

Mistress Maimuna could sense Mohammed's eyes on her ass and smiled. The brother craved her, and she would put him through hell before letting him get a taste of her goodies...

"Eat this ass, Mohammed, put that mouth to better use," Mistress Maimuna commanded as she squatted over Mohammed's face, after making the big and tall young Black man lie on the carpeted floor, stark naked.

Mohammed did as he was told, and admired her thick dark brown booty before sliding his tongue up her butt hole.

Mistress Maimuna smothered Mohammed's face with her ass, and smiled to herself. For she loved the feel of his tongue in the depths of her asshole...

"Yummy," Mohammed said, licking his lips after Mistress Maimuna rose from his face, pleased by the tongue bath he'd given her butt hole.

Mistress Maimuna looked at Mohammed and smiled, and then ordered him to get on all fours. With her gloved fingers she spread his ass cheeks and began fingering him.

Mohammed's butt hole tensed and quivered as Mistress Maimuna slid her tongue inside, and that's when she knew she had him...

"Mohammed, that ass belongs to me," Mistress Maimuna stated, and she stroked the burly Black man's big dick while fingering and licking his asshole.

Soon Mohammed began moaning and groaning. Mistress Maimuna lubricated him with Aveeno cream bought from the Dollar Store, and then pulled a sleek silvery strap-on dildo from her purse.

Without further ado, Mistress Maimuna pushed the dildo up Mohammed's ass, and the big dude cried out as she penetrated him...

"Oh damn," Mohammed squealed, and Mistress Maimuna gripped his hips tightly and thrust into him.

After working as an amateur dominatrix for ages, Maimuna had enjoyed dominating men of all races. Latino guys. White guys. Asian guys. Jewish guys. Filipino guys.

The only men Maimuna didn't have any luck with were Muslim men. This was much to the proud Muslim dominatrix's chagrin, of course.

The Muslim brothers simply refused to give into Maimuna's dominant ways, frustrating the hell out of the young Arab Muslim dominatrix.

Now, at last, Mistress Maimuna's ultimate fantasy was coming true. She got to top a strong Black Muslim man...

"Give up that precious Black ass, mister man," Mistress Maimuna cooed, holding Mohammed's arms behind his back while pounding her dildo into his ass.

Judging by how hard the brother's dick got, he really enjoyed having her torment and dominate him.

Mistress Maimuna fucked Mohammed Adewale's ass until the big man came and squealed, not screamed, mind you, but positively squealed.

196

It was absolutely sweet music to her ears. Only then did Mistress Maimuna pull her dildo out of his spent ass...

"Damn, now I'm horny," Mohammed said, stroking his still-hard dick while watching Maimuna put away the used, dirty dildo.

The young woman turned to look at him, and her eyes hungrily followed the motion of his hand pumping his dick.

Without a word, Maimuna pushed Mohammed down on the floor and straddled him. Her sleek hands went straight for his dick...

"I need some D," Maimuna said, and an amazed Mohammed looked on as she took his dick into her mouth and began sucking him off.

Hot damn, the feisty young woman's freakiness seemingly knew no bounds, and as far as

197

Mohammed was concerned, this was more than okay.

Bucking his hips, he thrust his dick down Maimuna's throat, and the young woman greedily sucked him off.

This was getting to be lots of fun. Maimuna sucked Mohammed until he came, and when he did, she slurped every last drop of his cum...

"I know you want this pussy but you haven't earned it yet," Maimuna said, fingering her wet pussy while Mohammed Adewale looked at her, hungrily.

"Thank you for showing me a brand new world," Mohammed said to Maimuna, after they got cleaned up. Maimuna smiled and thanked him in her own way.

198

The two of them shared a passionate kiss, and then went upstairs to continue with their fun. When they returned to work, smiling and enjoying each other's company, people were still surprised.

Maimuna Ali and Mohammed Adewale found that puzzling, but didn't let it bother them. Real Black men love strong Black women. What could be wrong with that ?

ON THE ISLAND

Lying on a straw mat next to the man she loves, Amina Al-Mahdi ran her hand over his chest, caressing his smooth, dark brown skin.

199

"What on earth are you thinking ?" her lover Achilles asked with a smile, and Amina simply shrugged.

"I'm thinking of the old country, you know, the Kingdom of Saudi Arabia," Amina said, sighing deeply.

"For me, home is right here with you," Achilles said, kissing her on the forehead. Amina smiled contentedly.

"Well said, my love, oh my, Achilles, you really do have a way with words, Mr. Jamaica," Amina said, laughing.

Absentmindedly Amina looked at the stars above. They glistened in the dark sky. For the thousandth time Amina tried to see the constellations she grew up watching.

Under the Saudi Arabian sky, out in the desert, Amina had often gone stargazing with her older brothers Omar and Yousef back in the day.

A passion for all things interstellar or cosmic, it's what led Amina to go so far from home, on the journey of a lifetime.

It compelled Amina to leave her hometown of Yanbu, in the Al Madinah province of Saudi Arabia for the extremely strange world of Ontario, Canada.

Amina had gone to study astrophysics at York University, right outside the City of Toronto. Little did Amina know how much her time in Canada would irreversibly change her.

For a young woman born and raised in rural Saudi Arabia, Canada was as different as could be. Almost like another world, actually.

At the Toronto International Airport she saw women in police uniforms, and even a female soldier.

In this strange society men and women mingled freely and seemed very affectionate with one another in public.

In the chaste, pious and strict world of Saudi Arabia, this Haram behavior simply wasn't allowed.

The women in Canada went around unveiled, indeed some went around almost half-naked, and everyone seemed to be just fine with that.

For in this country they were ruled by secular, humanitarian laws heavily influenced by the Women's Rights Movement, the polar opposite of Sharia Law.

Her first days in this strange country where women drove cars and went around unescorted by male chaperones were confusing, to say the least.

Nevertheless, Amina was determined to make the most of her time in Canada. This country was a dream come true for her.

It hadn't been easy to convince her tradition-minded father, Hassan Al-Mahdi, to allow her to go to Canada to study.

The venerable old Sheikh had worried that the Western world would change his only daughter so much that she would never want to come back to her native land.

"Amina, my sweet, I must warn you, the West is like another planet," her father cautiously warned.

203

Amina had insisted that the benefits of a Western University education outweighed the risks and the old man had to agree.

"Father, think of what I'll be able to accomplish with a Western education," Amina said, and the old man sighed and nodded.

In the Kingdom of Saudi Arabia, educated women were indeed an economic force to reckon with.

To the point that King Abdullah himself agreed to build all-female industrial cities for Saudi women workers.

Amina's father disagreed with the Great King as did many Saudi Arabian clerics but he kept his mouth shut.

The Al-Mahdi family patriarch sighed and looked into the dark eyes of his smart-mouthed, argumentative daughter.

The five-foot-ten, plump young woman whom the old preacher raised alone since her mother died giving birth to her, and given her his blessing to study abroad, though he hated to see her go.

"Bismillah, go with the grace of Allah, I wish you the best my angel," Amina's father said, and his joyful daughter embraced him.

All birds must leave the nest someday, Sheikh Hassan Al-Mahdi had mused while pondering his decision.

Now it was his eighteen-year-old daughter Amina's turn to leave the nest, spread her wings and fly away.

Her two older brothers Yousef and Omar were already married and had produced grandsons and granddaughters.

Soon it would be Amina's turn. Since she was going to be married soon, why not let her see a bit of the world ?

He didn't see any harm coming out of it. For he raised her well. *If only he knew.* Throughout her first month in provincial Ontario, Amina was truly homesick.

Amina watched TV, ate, did her prayers, read paperback romance novels and seldom left the house.

When September came Amina began her courses at York University, and thus the strangest and most wonderful time of her life began.

At York University, Amina Al-Mahdi met the two people destined to change her life forever.

The first one was a tall, slender young Jamaican-born Black Canadian woman named Persia Johnson.

The second one, none other than her boyfriend, a Turkish-born Russian Muslim émigré named Ferit Romanov.

Persia Johnson ran track and field for York University and Ferit was on the University of Toronto men's varsity soccer team.

The two student-athletes met at an Inter-Collegiate Athletics Community event and sparks simply flew between them.

The happy couple had been dating for well over a year at the time that Persia and Amina met.

Persia and Amina had the same major and were in some of the same classes.

The two of them became friends and Persia introduced Amina to her boyfriend Ferit Romanov.

The tall, spiky-haired Turkish man with the tattoos and Spiderman T-shirt didn't even register as a Muslim to Amina's eyes.

Nevertheless, she'd learned that most foreign Muslims were liberal when compared to a Saudi Arabian national.

The fact that Ferit, a young Muslim man from Turkey owned a dog and dated a Christian gal like Persia Johnson also surprised Amina but she took it in stride.

The world outside the Kingdom of Saudi Arabia was a strange place indeed, Amina admitted as much to herself.

Fortunately, Persia and Ferit became her guides and indeed her only friends at school for a while.

"Trust me, my dearest Amina, Toronto is going to rock your socks," Persia promised, and Amina nodded.

"You're never going to want to leave, Amina," Ferit said, nodding at Persia, who smiled at Amina knowingly.

"Thanks for being my guides," Amina said, and impulsively hugged them both. Persia and Ferit seemed surprised, but hugged her back.

Thanks to them Amina stopped spending so much time at the school library or in her apartment and actually went outside.

They showed her the environs of metropolitan York, which, while a fine town, couldn't hold a candle to the City of Toronto itself.

Amina, who grew up in a tiny rural town, found herself intimidated by the size and scope of Toronto at first but with her pal Persia's encouragement she came to see it as a challenge.

"Go out and explore the world, Amina, take chances and don't be such a chicken," Persia chided her.

Amina heeded her friend's advice, and actually enjoyed herself when she went out. And she didn't regret it.

Amina fell in love with the City of Toronto, where so many people of diverse races and ethnicities mingled freely.

Amina ate some delicious rice and beans in Jamaican restaurants, for she truly loved their enchanting food.

Oh, and Amina regularly prayed at a Masjid where eighty percent of the attendees were Somali, and she even became fascinated by Rap music, much to Persia's delight.

Amina's friendship with Ferit and Persia was changing her. Back in Saudi Arabia and much of the Arab world, Blacks were considered an inferior group, good only for labor.

Yet after knowing Persia and some of the Jamaican students at York University, Amina realized how wrong she'd been.

211

Black people were friendly, easygoing, good-hearted and God-fearing. A decent lot for the most part.

The Prophet Mohammed was right when he said the Black man was nobody's inferior in one of his more famous Hadiths.

Yes, her time in Canada had been strange, at times confusing but ultimately wonderful, Amina Al-Mahdi had to admit.

Amina aced her classes at York University, but when summer came, she felt a pang of regret at leaving the campus and town which felt like home.

"Come back to us when you can, sister, we will miss you always," Persia said, giving Amina a fierce hug at the airport.

"Amina, I swear this, I will miss you very much, my Saudi sister," Ferit said with a smile and nod.

The tall Turkish sportsman was quite surprised when Amina simply went up to him and hugged him.

Observant Muslim women didn't touch men they were unrelated to, even if they were of the same faith.

For a Saudi gal like Amina, who never left the house without her Hijab, long-sleeved shirt and long skirt, to hug Ferit, now that was really something.

"I will miss you both every day," Amina said tearfully as the final call for her flight rang out throughout the airport lane.

Smiling sadly, Amina waved her friends goodbye and boarded the plane. Time to go, whether she liked it or not.

Once inside, Amina went to her assigned seat by the window, sat down and then she tucked herself in.

The old White lady sitting next to her eyed her suspiciously. Ah, the joys of flying while Arab in the post 9/11 world.

Slowly Amina drifted into a deep sleep, and dreamed of the City of Toronto and her stalwart friends.

When Amina opened her eyes, the plane was going down, and everyone around her was screaming in a blind panic.

"What's going on ?" Amina asked the person sitting next to her, and the old White man shrugged nonchalantly.

The airplane was going down, that's all Amina could remember anyone saying. She'd been heading home, back to Saudi Arabia, on a long flight.

One that would take Amina from metropolitan Toronto, Ontario, to the City of London, England, and only once in Europe would she finally make her way to the Kingdom.

The world was a big place, much bigger than most people realized, and Amina Al-Mahdi was just beginning to explore it.

As the plane dropped out of the sky, Amina Al-Mahdi silently prayed to God that she might one day see her friends again.

215

Ferit and Persia meant much more to Amina than she let on. Her goodbyes had been slow and painful, and there was much she'd left unsaid.

The odd thing is that even as the plane fell out of the sky like a rock, all she could think of were her friends, her University and her old life in Toronto.

Amina hadn't had the heart to tell her friends the truth, that her father, the esteemed Sheikh Hassan Al-Mahdi had summoned her back to Saudi Arabia because a young man from a good family had requested her hand in marriage.

If everything went according to plan, Amina Al-Mahdi would never set foot in Ontario, Canada, again.

Amina would become the wife of some wealthy young Saudi Arabian businessman and henceforth her only preoccupations would be wifedom and motherhood.

Such was the fate of all Saudi women, from the Princesses of the royal House of Saud to the lowly beggars.

Amina Al-Mahdi woke up slowly and painfully. When she opened her eyes, a dark face loomed over her.

Eyes widened with shock, Amina Al-Mahdi blurted out several phrases in Arabic before realizing that the dark-skinned young man couldn't understand her.

"Ma'am, um, do you speak any English?" the young man asked in an accent she vaguely recognized.

Amina nodded, slowly, still overwhelmed while taking it all in, and the young Black man introduced himself.

"Good morning, ma'am, hope you're okay, I'm Achilles Jackson," the stranger said gently, and Amina looked him up and down.

"You're Jamaican," Amina said, recognizing in his inflections something similar to the way her old friend Persia Johnson spoke.

"Yes, ma'am, I am indeed Jamaican. Very astute of you to notice. I was born and bred in Montego Bay," Achilles Johnson said proudly.

"Salaam, um, brother, pleased to meet you," Amina said, and Achilles nodded at her, an amused look on his face.

Thus Amina met the man who pulled out of the airplane wreck and dragged her to this beach, on a tiny island in the middle of nowhere.

"Where in hell are we, my friend ?" Amina asked her fellow survivor, and the young Jamaican shrugged.

"Sister, I swear, I honestly don't have a clue," Achilles said wistfully, and Amina sighed and shook her head.

"We are frigging screwed," Amina said, shrugging helplessly, and Achilles sighed and nodded in agreement.

It didn't take long for Amina and Achilles to realize the precarious nature of their situation. They were stuck on a desert island right in the middle of nowhere.

"Where in hell are we? What is this place?" Amina asked, glaring at Achilles, who stroked his goateed chin.

"I figured we're somewhere between North America and Europe," Achilles said when Amina repeatedly queried him on the subject.

The island, which seemed only about five kilometers long and two kilometers wide, had an abundance of fruitful trees and a couple of streams so they wouldn't starve or die of thirst.

Still, life on the island would be a struggle for survival at best for the two hapless, stranded castaways.

At first glance, Amina Al-Mahdi, first daughter of Sheikh Hassan Al-Mahdi of Al Madinah province, Saudi Arabia, had very little in common with a certain Jamaican-born Toronto College student/aspiring rapper named Achilles Jackson.

They were both air breathers and came from metropolitan Toronto, that's it. They had nothing else in common.

As they foraged the remains of the plane for anything they might use, the burly Jamaican's habit of whistling and singing got on Amina's last nerve.

Amina bit her lip, and lasted all of one hour before angrily telling Achilles to basically shut the fuck up.

"Achilles, um, must you really do that ?" Amina asked vehemently, and Achilles looked at her innocently.

When Amina said that, Achilles burst out laughing, and when she cocked an angry eyebrow at him, he told her she was the first Hijabi he'd heard cussing like a sailor.

Amina smiled, and told Achilles that the rumors of those precious Hijabis being soft and sweet were greatly exaggerated.

"People keep thing that women who wear the Hijab are submissive and soft but we're not," Amina said, sucking in her teeth.

"Oh, my dear, trust me, I can definitely believe that, I see the fire in your eyes," Achilles said thoughtfully, and Amina smiled.

"Well, Mr. Achilles, don't get burned," Amina said slyly, and Achilles held his hands up in mock surrender.

222

The first day proved to be one of the toughest, for they realized that they were stranded on the island, the sole survivors of a plane that crashed a mere six hundred meters from the beach, in shallow waters.

From the plane's wreck they found very little they could salvage, but Achilles was undaunted by their situation.

"Well, we can get definitely get our hands on some materials and then try and build ourselves a shelter," Achilles said thoughtfully.

"Achilles, you want me to believe you're an expert at this sort of thing ?" Amina asked, hands on her hips.

Achilles told Amina he would build them a shelter, but he needed her help. The task would be less arduous with two pairs of hands...

223

"I need your help on this, Amina, for real, I can't do this alone," Achilles said earnestly, and Amina nodded.

"Alright, Achilles, let's do this," Amina said simply, then laughed, amused by the shocked look on Achilles face.

The proud daughter of a rural Saudi preacher promised the Jamaican castaway that she wasn't afraid to get her hands dirty.

"You should know, I'm much tougher and more handy than I look, Mr. Jamaica," Amina said, and Achilles nodded.

"Well, my Saudi sister, this is indeed a day for surprises," Achilles said, marveling at her and grinning.

224

Amina was definitely a handy kind of gal. After all, her father had been too poor to hire many workers and she and her brothers often lent a hand around the family farm.

It took them three days of hard and tiresome labor but they built a hut out of wood, leaves and a thatch roof.

It wasn't much but it would do. As the days droned on, Amina and Achilles were forced to rely on one another.

They were each other's only hope for survival until they were rescued. There was no getting around that fact.

At least that's what Amina told herself. The situation looked bleak, but she was thankful for Achilles company.

Even though Achilles wasn't Muslim (the heavy-
looking silver crucifix hanging around his neck
made that clear) he was a   pretty decent man.

In Saudi Arabia,   rape and sexual harassment were
so prevalent that the   clerics   made it national law
that women   couldn't go anywhere without a   male
protector.

Westerners   believed that this was a way for Saudi
men to control their women but Amina   could see
both sides of the   coin as a Saudi woman.

There was a rape epidemic in Arab and North
African countries but this seldom made news
since everyone was so busy talking about oil
prospectors, interfaith conflicts and terrorists,
often in the same breath.

In many ways, Achilles surprised Amina. He was always polite and friendly when dealing with her, though he was sarcastic and brutally honest.

"Amina, I need you as badly as you need me to survive out here, but your attitude needs work," Achilles said bluntly to her one morning.

"I'm all about respect but I'm not in love with your tone," Amina shot back. Achilles was starting to annoy her.

"Whatever," Achilles mumbled, looking her up and down before walking away. *Such a prima donna this Amina*, he thought.

Amina watched Achilles go, then the young Saudi Arabian Muslim woman looked down at herself, sighing.

The long-sleeved T-shirt and long skirt Amina had been wearing when flying comprised the sum of her belongings, and it wouldn't be long before they became rags.

The Jamaican didn't see anything wrong with walking around in his boxer shorts and T-shirt, since the silk pants and Black leather jacket he'd been wearing on the flight were ill-suited for island life.

In spite of herself, Amina noted that Achilles was good-looking, albeit in a very rough and rugged kind of way.

Achilles reminded Amina of the Mauritanian construction workers she'd once seen in an oil plant while visiting the Capital province.

The Mauritanians, with their unique blend of African and Arabian bloodlines, were a beautiful people.

Of course, none of them swore as much as Achilles did, that's for sure. Amina slowly got used to his profanity. The brother should have been a sailor...

"Mr. Achilles of Jamaica, he of the great physique and extremely foul mouth," Amina said to herself, laughing.

Achilles sighed as he rested under a tree, slowly catching his breath after swimming in the ocean for a bit.

The waters surrounding the island weren't as warm as those of his beloved Jamaica but they would do fine, for the duration.

"Got to make the best of a bad situation, at the end of the day, that's all any man can do," Achilles quietly told himself.

He'd invited Amina to go for a swim but the young Saudi woman declined, something about modesty and propriety, blah.

Achilles had simply rolled his eyes at Little Miss Religious and gone into the water. Amina watched him on the beach, before going deeper into the woods to forage for fruit.

Achilles, an expert swimmer, had gone pretty far out into the ocean, almost a kilometer from shore, before heading back to the island.

Achilles emerged from the surf half a kilometer from the beach where they'd made camp, feeling refreshed.

Lying there under the tree, Achilles found himself growing a bit sleepy, for swimming was a tiring endeavor, but something moving in the beach caught his eye. *It was Amina.*

The young Saudi Arabian woman stood about ten feet from the water, and looked at the surf. The blue waves were tempting.

Amina hesitated, then began undressing. Off came the long-sleeved T-shirt, then her long skirt, followed by her underwear.

"Oh my," Achilles whispered, and the young man found himself quite simply mesmerized by what he was beholding.

Naked, Amina stood on the beach, a tall, curvy and lovely young woman with dark bronze skin and raven hair.

The sight of Amina in her birthday suit stirred an all too familiar longing deep within the loins of Achilles.

Achilles watched as the lovely, curvaceous Amina tentatively set foot into the water, then went inside.

Giggling like a schoolgirl, Amina went deeper into the surf. Achilles watched her intently. He'd never seen anything so beautiful.

If the average Saudi Arabian women were half as beautiful as Amina, Achilles understood why their men made them cover up. *Hot damn !*

"Dammit, that woman has one hell of a booty, one of the best I've seen," Achilles whispered to himself, amazed.

Amina had a thick round ass like an island mama, and as a Jamaican man Achilles would totally know !

Achilles watched as Amina went deeper and deeper into the water, frolicking among the waves and enjoying herself with an innocence that was touching.

The sight of Amina turned him on immensely. Achilles felt himself harden, and felt slightly guilty. He really shouldn't be doing this...

Amina was so sweet and innocent, Achilles could see that, even when she tried to act tough and pushy.

A shriek snapped Achilles out of his lustful daydream, and he gasped in shock. What's going on here ?

233

Achilles blinked when he saw Amina splashing about in the surf. Like Venus rising from the waves. *What the fuck ?*

Amina was drowning! Achilles leapt to his feet and rushed headlong into the beach, before wading into the waves.

"Hang on, hang in there, Amina, hold on for a second, I'm coming !" Achilles screamed, and he raced towards her.

Kicking furiously, moving as fast as he could, Achilles waded through the waves and made his way toward Amina.

"God don't let me be too late," Achilles prayed silently, watching Amina flounder as he neared her.

Her resistance proved futile and Amina fell beneath the waves. Achilles obligingly dove under to reach her.

Achilles caught Amina's floundering form, and through sheer effort, he brought her back to the surface.

"I've got you, my dear, don't worry," Achilles said, holding onto the lovely Amina tightly as he possibly could.

Clasping Amina in his arms, Achilles carried her to the beach, laid her on the soft sand. Hot damn, Amina was even better-looking up close, Achilles remarked.

Big, firm breasts, wide shoulders, a round belly, wide hips, thick legs, and that derriere. Amina was something else.

"Focus," Achilles told himself, as he brought his lips to Amina's, to perform mouth-to-mouth resuscitation.

Achilles pressed his hands against Amina's chest, and slammed his fist there, then breathed into her mouth again.

"Come on, come back to me, Amina, you survived the plane crash, don't die like this," Achilles said, his voice sounding pitiful even to his ears.

The lovely Amina wasn't moving. At all. Nor was she breathing. Achilles looked heavenward, and sighed.

"Please God let her live, I'll do anything," Achilles said, bowing deeply and shaking his head in despair.

Once more Achilles breathed into Amina's mouth while pressing down on her chest. The young woman began to stir...

Moments later, Amina's brown eyes snapped open and then she shuddered while vomiting violently.

Amina looked around, a bit haggard, panic in her eyes. The young woman was clearly still quite disoriented.

"Achilles, where in hell am I ? Um, what's going on ?" Amina asked, a panicked look on her rather lovely face.

"You're safe now Amina," Achilles told her with a wan smile. This chick was starting to get on his nerves...

A little while later, a fully dressed but still shaken Amina sat across from the concerned Achilles.

"You really shouldn't go swimming alone milady," Achilles told her, smiling faintly and Amina firmly nodded.

"Um, Achilles, thanks, I guess I really do owe you a thank you for saving me," Amina said hesitantly, and Achilles nodded.

Achilles smirked, and reminded Amina how lucky she was that he was around. Amina nodded, smiled a little and then suspicion flared in her lovely brown eyes.

"One thing has been bugging me, Achilles, how did you come by so fast ?" Amina asked, her eyes narrowed to slits.

"Um, no big deal, Amina, really, you see, I just happened to be nearby," Achilles began, his voice nervous.

Anger contorted Amina's beautiful features, and Achilles bit his lips. The lady looked good while angry...

"Achilles ! You were spying on me," Amina said through gritted teeth, and Achilles shook his head but said nothing.

Standing up, Amina glared at him angrily. Achilles matched her angry stare. Seriously, what was her problem ?

"Not exactly," Achilles said weakly, and Amina shot him a wuthering look. *If only he could make her understand...*

Achilles took a step toward Amina, meaning to apologize, but she apparently took it the wrong way.

Achilles felt the ringing slap on his cheek that sounded out like thunder to his ears. Achilles rubbed his cheek, and then Amina was suddenly gone in a huff.

Rubbing his cheek slowly, Achilles watched Amina go. *Damn this Saudi Arabian woman had an ass on her !*

That night Achilles slept alone in the hut, thinking about the day's events. His balls were bluer than the northern sky.

The next day, Achilles went looking for Amina. Time to sort things out. He had to make peace with her. They were the only people on the island...

240

Achilles found Amina further down the beach, with a makeshift basket full of fruits, and his stomach grumbled loudly.

"Well, Achilles, good morning to you, now, what do you want ?" Amina asked, her eyes filled with suspicion.

"Lady, hold your horses. Seriously. I didn't like the way things went down last night. I'm here to make peace," Achilles said softly.

"Achillles, please come. It is I who should apologize," Amina said, and when those words left her lips, Achilles froze, stunned.

If lightning had come down from the skies and struck him right then and there, then Achilles wouldn't have been more shocked.

"You saved my life back there and I thank Allah for your help," Amina conceded, and she smiled sheepishly.

"Amina, I wasn't spying on you, you see, I was just sleeping under a coconut tree when you went into the water," Achilles offered.

Amina shot him a look, then smiled. Achilles smiled back, and shrugged. To Amina's surprise, the handsome brother appeared to be blushing.

"Mighty Achilles, Hmm, I guess I woke you up, huh ?" Amina said with a wry grin, chiding him and Achilles nodded.

Pleased to see Amina relax at last, Achilles shrugged and smiled. *The lady doth have a nice smile,* he thought.

"Amina, at the end of the day, I'm only human, you seem to forget that," Achilles said with a cocky grin.

"Come, my friend, enough talk, let's eat," Amina said evenly, gesturing to the basket, and Achilles nodded.

The two of them shared the fruits, then sat down and talked. They'd been on the island for seventeen days now.

Now, Amina and Achilles had ample fruits and plenty of water to subsist on, there would come a day when they would have to find other sources of food.

"What else can we do ? One day we are going to run out of fruit," Amina said, and Achilles nodded thoughtfully.

243

"My dear Amina, one of these days, I'm going to take the time to teach you how to fish," Achilles said.

Amina laughed at that. The idea of a College man and wannabe rapper like Achilles fishing amused her.

"Lady, look, you shouldn't mock fishermen. My father is a fisherman you know," Achilles said defensively.

Seeing his expression, Amina apologized. Apparently, Achilles had taken her laugh the wrong way.

"Achilles, my friend, I honestly didn't mean to offend you," Amina said, gently touching his muscular arm.

Achilles looked at her hand on his, and the young man held his breath. *What is he thinking ?* Amina wondered.

The whole time they'd been together on the island Amina had kept him at arm's length, Achilles was well aware of that.

Amina looked at Achilles, and when her skin touched his, she felt something akin to an electrical shock and her heart thundered in her chest.

"Brother Achilles, oh my, I'm really sorry for touching you, I had no right," Amina said, shaking her head.

Achilles leaned closer to her. Amina looked at him, her eyes filled with wonder...eager and scared of what was about to happen.

245

"Amina, please don't be sorry," Achilles said softly, and Amina's worried expression turned into a smile. Then he kissed her.

Much to Achilles immense surprise, Amina kissed him back. Gently, Achilles pulled Amina into his arms and kissed her full and deep.

"I shouldn't do this," Amina said hesitantly when they came up for air, and Achilles shook his head firmly.

"Amina, you're beautiful and I've wanted you from the first time I saw you, and it's perfectly natural," Achilles countered.

When Amina heard that, the young Saudi Arabian woman smiled and blushed. No one had ever spoken to her in this manner.

246

"Really ? You truly find me beautiful ?" Amina asked hesitantly, stunned by Achilles words, for she sensed he meant them.

Achilles nodded sagely, and Amina looked into his eyes thoughtfully. This man was unlike any she'd ever known.

"Um, Achilles, I have something to confess, you see, I'm a virgin, Amina said softly, then added, "I don't know how to make love."

Silencing Amina with a kiss, Achilles stopped her. The young woman sighed happily, and embraced him.

"Amina, my dear, let me take care of you," Achilles whispered into her ear, and Amina smiled and nodded.

Gently Achilles laid Amina on the straw bed, and slowly undressed her.

Like many curvy women, Amina was a bit self-conscious about her body but Achilles, who worshipped big beautiful women of all races, assured her that she was lovely.

"Amina, believe me, you're one of the loveliest women I've ever seen," Achilles said earnestly, and Amina smiled.

"Thank you, you crazy handsome man," Amina whispered, and then she kissed Achilles once again.

Looking into Amina's lovely eyes, Achilles assured her that he wouldn't hurt her. It was the furthest thing from his mind.

Gently Achilles kissed her forehead, her eyes, her lips. He kissed Amina's neck and she giggled softly.

"That tickles, I like it," Amina said, nodding approvingly and Achilles grinned, and continued what he was doing.

Achilles kissed Amina's breasts, suckling on the surprisingly large areolas of her tits. Such a lovely woman.

"So damn beautiful," Achilles paused to whisper, as he continued pleasuring Amina. The young woman began to relax a bit...

Amina licked her lips as Achilles totally went to work on her. The Jamaican stud kissed a path down her lovely body, from her breasts to her round belly.

249

Achilles flicked his tongue into her belly button and Amina laughed. He made his way to her pelvic area, and spread her big, sexy legs.

"Achilles, what are you doing?" Amina asked nervously, and Achilles took a deep breath, then smiled at her.

Amina clamped her legs shut, halting his progress, and Achilles looked into her beautiful, worried face.

"Will it hurt? Please, let me know, I can take it, I think," Amina said softly. Her lovely face was full of uncertainty.

"Amina, relax, I will only bring you pleasure, my dear, this much I promise you," Achilles assured Amina.

250

The young Saudi Arabian woman took a deep breath, then nodded and relaxed.

Once more Achilles spread Amina's thick, sexy legs, and looked at her hairy pussy. She was already wet, which made him smile.

"Go ahead," Amina whispered, and Achilles smiled thankfully, then nodded. Amina lay on the bed, tense from head to toe as Achilles played with her pussy.

"You taste wonderful," Achilles whispered, and Amina smiled at him. Sensations she'd never experienced filled her being.

Conflicting feelings warred within Amina's mind even as Achilles pleasured her body in his weirdly wonderful way.

A proper and decent Muslim woman should only expose her Awrah (the Arabic word for a lady's private parts) around her husband and no one else.

Islamic law was one hundred percent adamant about that last bit. No nookie before the wedding night...

And here Amina was, allowing herself to be touched intimately and pleasured by Achilles, a man who clearly wasn't her husband.

Hell, Achilles wasn't even Muslim! This was unacceptable. Amina shouldn't be doing this and she knew it.

Yet, Amina's body cried out for his strong yet gentle touch and she knew it. She ached for Achilles.

Achilles gently slid his tongue into Amina's sweet pussy, and the young Saudi woman cried out sharply.

"I'm going to give you the Jamaican special," Achilles warned Amina before burying his face between her legs.

As Achilles tongue slid deep into her pussy, followed by his agile fingers, Amina cried out in pleasure.

"Wow, hmm, Achilles, that's so damn intense," Amina said, moaning softly as Achilles toyed with her pussy.

Places within Amina that had never been touched became filled with pleasure as they were explored and pleased at last.

Orgasmic for the first time in her life, Amina cried out in every language she knew, including Arabic, Farsi and English !

Amina lay on the bed, panting and moaning, her body covered in a shine fine of sweat, and for a moment, she wasn't sure where she was.

Then the lovely Amina remembered. She was on the island, lying in her handsome lover Achilles strong and loving arms.

"What in hell was that ?" Amina asked breathlessly, and Achilles smiled at her. This gal hadn't felt anything yet.

"Jamaican magic my angel, I can definitely show you more if you want," Achilles said with a knowing grin.

"That was amazing," Amina said, and she looked at Achilles, her soulful brown eyes filled with sheer wonder.

"Well, my dear Amina, let me know if you want to see the second act," Achilles said, and smiled for effect.

Amina nodded, and watched as the Jamaican stud stroked his long and thick, uncircumcised member.

Her eyes widened at the size of it. Amina had never seen one quite like Achilles. The brother was...gifted.

"Achilles, can I touch it please ?" Amina said, reaching out tentatively. Achilles was pleased by her reaction.

The young man smiled at her and nodded firmly. *If only Amina knew how badly Achilles craved her touch...*

Achilles held his breath as Amina gently ran her hands all over his dick. Looking him in the eyes, dead-serious, Amina told him she wanted him inside of her.

"Now," Amina said sharply, and Achilles grinned, pleased by the eagerness in her tone. She really wanted it...

"Yes ma'am," Achilles said with a grin that threatened to split his face. How he yearned for Amina...

Amina looked up at Achilles as he got on top of her. *This is it,* she thought. The moment of truth had come.

256

Amina tenderly rapped her arms around Achilles, and once more he kissed her. Gently Achilles licked Amina's breasts while spreading her thick, sexy legs.

"Relax my angel," Achilles whispered, and Amina nodded, then did as he asked. Locking eyes with Achilles, Amina opened herself up to him, wanting to feel him inside of her.

For part of her ached for his touch. Achilles looked into Amina's lovely brown eyes as he rubbed his hard dick against her hairy mound.

"Are you ready ?" Achilles asked her gently. Amina licked her lips and nodded. This gal was something else...

Achilles smiled at her, pleased by Amina's resolve. Perhaps this hard-headed Saudi woman could finally listen to reason.

257

"If you want it come and get it, I'm ready for you," Amina said teasingly, locking eyes with Achilles.

"Oh it's like that, huh?" Achilles said, as he eased himself inside of her. A sharp cry escaped Amina's lips as Achilles swiftly penetrated her.

Achilles asked Amina if she was okay and the young Saudi woman nodded. She yearned to feel all of him inside of her.

Achilles pushed himself deeper inside of Amina. Never before had he been with anyone half as tight.

Burying his face between Amina's voluminous breasts, Achilles thrust his dick deeper inside of her.

"Oh damn," Amina squealed, and Achilles began fucking her with gusto. Amina's moans filled the air, echoed by Achilles groans of pleasure.

"You're an amazing woman," Achilles said, kissing Amina on the forehead. The young woman looked at him, an almost feral gleam in her eyes.

"Thank you, now fuck me harder," Amina cried out, and Achilles smiled. Gently, roughly, passionately, they made love. And didn't stop until the wee hours of the morning.

The next morning proved somewhat awkward for the two lovebirds. The morning after is indeed known for its awkwardness...

Only in the cold light of day did Amina Al-Mahdi consider the full ramifications of everything she and Achilles Jackson had done the previous night.

Amina was an unmarried Muslim woman who had sex with a man who wasn't her husband.

In the Kingdom of Saudi Arabia, Amina's family awaited, along with a suitor, someone chosen by her father Hassan Al-Mahdi to be her future husband.

According to Islamic Law, Amina knew she would be put to death in Saudi Arabia for what she'd done.

In the Kingdom of Saudi Arabia, any Muslim woman who had sex with a man she wasn't married to would be put to death.

As was the late, great Princess Misha'al bint Fahd al Saud in the fateful, deadly summer of 1977. The summer the Saudi Kingdom executed a princess.

If and when Amina returned to Saudi Arabia, and it was discovered that she'd lost her virginity, she knew she would be surely put to death.

Despair and guilt sagged the young Saudi Arabian Muslim woman's shoulders. What on earth was she to do ?

Achilles woke up next to Amina, and the sight of her beautiful face and lovely body so close to his thrilled him.

"Hello beautiful," Achilles said, his eyes roving up and down Amina's lovely form. Such raw beauty, he thought.

In his twenty four years upon this earth, Achilles had been with Jamaican women, Ethiopian women, Hispanic women, Chinese women and of course White women.

Lovely ladies of all hues flocked to the Jamaican man, since his reputation as a lover was absolutely legendary.

And yet, Achilles had never been with anyone as lovely as Amina. Amina wasn't like the others. Achilles knew this deep in his bones.

Who knew the Hijab-wearing pious and studious young Muslim woman from Saudi Arabia had such passion in her ?

Amina was the kind of woman who could effortlessly tame Achilles wild ways if he wasn't careful.

The kind of woman a man brings home to mama. If he's real smart, that is. Since Achilles woke up before Amina, he decided to take care of business.

The young Jamaican stud went to take a dump, swam in the ocean a bit and then got dressed before foraging for fruits.

Achilles found plenty of fruit, and brought a basketful back to Amina. Perhaps this would cheer her up...

For a while, Achilles searched for Amina. He found her sitting on the straw bed, pensive. Clearing his throat, he stepped closer.

"Good morning sunshine," Achilles said with a smile, and he looked at Amina, who gazed upon him adoringly.

Amina looked him up and down, smiled faintly and paused, a strange expression on her lovely face.

"Hi Achilles," Amina said meekly, and the young man's heart sank. *Oh yeah, I think I smell trouble,* Achilles thought.

Amina smiled hesitantly as Achilles sat next to her, and reached for her hand. Amina batted his hand away.

"Look, Achilles, um, we shouldn't have done what we did last night," Amina said, biting her lip, and Achilles paused.

"Why not ?" asked Achilles, speaking softly, feeling quite honestly puzzled by Amina's drastic behavioral change.

Amina vigorously shook her head. *How could she hope to make Achilles understand her people's strange and unique ways ?*

"Achilles, I'm a Muslim woman and you're a Christian, it could never work out," Amina said with a deep sigh.

Shrugging, Amina added that they came from completely different worlds. In more ways than she cared to explain.

"I am sorry, Achilles, but that's the way it has to be," Amina said sadly. Achilles shook his head, and stroked his beard. *This requires careful handling,* he thought.

"Amina, I think I've got feelings for you," Achilles said, meaning it. Gently Achilles touched Amina's long, curly Black hair, and she shrank from his touch.

Seeing the hurt in Achilles soulful brown eyes, Amina winced and swiftly apologized. Hurting him wasn't her intent.

"Achilles, look, um, I don't want to cause you pain but this is not going to work out," Amina said softly.

Achilles took a deep breath. *All of a sudden, he knew what he had to do. Great sacrifices must be made in the name of love.*

"When we get back to civilization I will convert to Islam and ask your family for your hand in marriage," Achilles said earnestly.

Amina stared at him, stunned. Looking into Achilles eyes, she saw that he was absolutely sincere.

"*Achilles*, my friend, *I don't want you to convert*," Amina said at last. Achilles sighed. What does this woman want ?

"Achilles, you don't know the first thing about Saudi society. Even if you do, my family is racist, most Arabs are," Amina added.

"Explain this to me," Achilles said, folding his arms, and Amina sighed. This wasn't going to be easy at all...

"In the Arab world the men can marry women of any race or faith but us Muslim women can only marry men from our own cultures and religion," Amina stated matter-of-factly.

"I guess that's why I've never seen a Black Muslim man with an Arab woman," Achilles said, smiling wistfully.

"Interracial relationships are complex the world over," Amina said defensively. She didn't want to think of her Saudi homeland as a racist place.

" I guess you Arabs think we're not good enough for you, we the people of Africa and the Caribbean," Achilles said angrily.

There was a world of bitterness in his eyes. *The pain in Achilles's eyes made Amina wince. She turned away.*

"Achilles, many of my people are racist against Blacks, that's true, but I'm not like that," Amina said evenly.

Shaking his head, Achilles got up and walked away, shoulders slumped. "Whatever," Achilles called out, over his shoulder, as he walked away.

Achilles couldn't stand to be near Amina all of a sudden. Lest he do or say something they'd both regret.

Sitting on the straw mat that served as their bed, Amina bit her fingernails, something she did often when angry, saddened or outraged.

No man had ever made Amina feel like Achilles had. He'd been wonderful, patient, kind and respectful to her.

In Amina's entire existence, no one had ever wanted to know who she was inside. *Or share their true selves with her.* Nope.

They simply assumed they knew her because of her gender, faith and culture. And most of the time they were wrong.

Achilles wasn't like the others. He told Amina pretty much everything there was to know about himself.

Born in Montego Bay, Jamaica, Achilles moved to Toronto, Ontario, with his family during his first year of high school.

After a failed career as part of a Rap group, Achilles had been taking criminal justice courses at Seneca College before he ended in this predicament....

Achilles studied at Seneca College in preparation for a career in law enforcement in any Canadian town or city that would hire him.

The young man had been contemplating summer school when his aunt Giselle in London, UK, sent him tickets to come spend the summer with her.

Achilles had never been to the U.K. and was thrilled about visiting London, England. *Of course, it was not to be.*

The plane in which Achilles was went down, and he found himself stuck on a desert island with a hot but uptight and humorless Muslim woman. Great.

Amina thought of her old life back in the Kingdom of Saudi Arabia. She had changed so much since...

Although Amina's father and brothers were always nice to her, she'd led a lonely existence, unable to live the house without a male chaperone like all women inside the Kingdom.

Oh, and Amina had no female companions, for her father Hassan Al-Mahdi had no female siblings and neither did she.

Amina Al-Mahdi's life back home was quite complicated, and boring, and at times she felt restless.

271

That's why Amina wanted to attend University in another country. *Sometimes, although she loved her country, Saudi Arabia felt like a prison to Amina.*

During that one amazing year Amina spent in the province of Ontario, Canada, her life changed completely.

Her friendship with Persia Johnson and Ferit Romanov, her wanderings around York and Toronto, her visits to museums, sporting events and zoos had changed her life.

In Canada Amina Al-Mahdi felt like anything was possible. Absolutely anything.

In Ontario where Amina studied, a lesbian woman got elected as the political leader of the entire province.

In Canada a woman could be virtually anything she wanted to be. In Saudi Arabia a woman was little more than expensive livestock.

Try as she might, Amina Al-Mahdi couldn't deny it. The Kingdom of Saudi Arabia was rather...strict on women.

Sometimes, while hanging out in Persia Johnson's apartment, Amina felt jealous when her best friend talked about her boyfriend Ferit Romanov and how much she loved him.

"You are so lucky to have him," Amina once told Persia, and the lovely young Jamaican woman smiled.

"Thank you, Amina, Wallahi, my dear Ferit is the only man I've ever loved," Persia said with a big grin.

273

The two of them always seemed so happy together. It was clear to Amina that Ferit absolutely cherished Persia.

Would she ever get to experience such joy? Amina strongly doubted it. Her life would be one of modesty, seclusion and devotion...

In the Kingdom of Saudi Arabia marriages were the norm, women were expected to produce children, that's it.

No need for love between husband and wife. It's a nice thing to have but it's not necessary, that's how the mullahs felt.

Amina's heart twisted in pain as she thought of that. *Such were the fates of all women like her, inside the Kingdom.*

Of course, Amina Al-Mahdi would never admit such a thing out loud. Still, she admitted it to herself...

In the Kingdom of Saudi Arabia, where arranged marriages were a matter of law and culture. Marriage for love was unheard of.

Saudi Arabian women dared not dream of love, at least not within the same context as Western women.

Living with a man who bedded and wedded their body but not their soul, such was the fate of virtually all Saudi women.

Amina Al-Mahdi dared not dream of love, and certainly not the passionate kind she'd seen Persia and Ferit exhibit for one another.

275

"A love like yours is something I dare not dream of for myself," Amina said to Persia, who hugged her fiercely.

"Have faith, Amina, trust me when I say that fate has good things in store for you," Persia gently told her.

Amina smiled wistfully, a certain warmth creeping into her chest as she thought of her best friend Persia and her old life in the City of Toronto.

Amina never dreamed such a thing could be possible for someone like her, a Hijab-wearing prim and proper, deeply traditional young Saudi woman, until she met Achilles Jackson.

"Love is not just precious and rare it's a force of nature," Amina remembered Persia saying once.

When Amina remembered that, the young woman actually closed her eyes, hard.

"How do you know Ferit is the one ?" Amina asked, and Persia actually laughed.

"The first time Ferit held me in his arms and made love to me, I felt truly alive, and then he told me he loved me," Persia said dreamily.

"Um, that's great, too much info, my dearest sister," Amina said, laughing and Persia smiled and shrugged.

In those days, Amina Al-Mahdi was pretty jaded about life, love and relationships. And then along came Achilles...

Amina Al-Mahdi had indeed found love, with a most unlikely man, against all odds...and she foolishly threw it away.

"Allah forgive me but I love this man," Amina said aloud, then the young woman took off in the direction that Achilles had gone.

Frantically Amina searched one end of the island then the other. She simply couldn't find Achilles anywhere.

A splash out in the surf caught Amina's attention, and she saw Achilles in the water, approximately two hundred meters from shore.

Damn he looked good, so tall and strong, his dark skin contrasting against the blue waves.

Suddenly filled with inspiration, Amina Al-Mahdi, prim and proper Saudi Muslim woman, kicked off her shoes.

So Achilles didn't want to speak to her, eh? *Well, Amina knew one sure fire way to get his full attention.*

"I really have to forget about this crazy woman and her weird culture," Achilles quietly told himself.

Foreign women are nothing but trouble. Actually, all women are trouble, come to think of it, Achilles thought bitterly.

Achilles dove under the waves, and resurfaced, letting the sea water fall off of him. The young Jamaican stud stood there, expecting to feel glorious and strong.

Instead the sadness Achilles felt since Amina's speech to him this morning dug at his heart like a crab's pincer through a fish's soft belly.

279

Looking heavenward, the young Jamaican immigrant silently asked God why He created women.

Women, indeed the most damnably confusing and indecisive creatures in the entire frigging cosmos, to be sure.

Did the Almighty design them to confuse men in a cosmic laboratory of sorts ? Sometimes it sure seems like it ! Why did they have to be so damn complicated ?

A splash in the waves caught Achilles attention. What the heck ? His eyes widened when he saw...*her.*

The tall, lovely and sinfully curvaceous Saudi Arabian Muslim gal waded into the surf, naked as a jay bird.

"Amina, what in hell are you doing in the water ?" Achilles asked, scratching his growing beard, a bit puzzled.

"As Salam Alaikum, greetings to you, my dearest Achilles," Amina said, laughing as she stepped forward.

Moving confidently, the lovely Amina Al-Mahdi made her way to him. A frisson ran through his spine, and Achilles shivered under the blazing sun.

"Achilles, my brother, I'm sorry for what I said earlier," Amina said, amorously pressing her gorgeous naked form against his.

Damn this broad, when she spoke to him like that he could forgive her anything. And they both knew it.

"Hmm, whatever happened to your people's sacrosanct traditions ?" Achilles asked her, still a bit cautious.

"I don't give a damn about tradition, I just want to be happy, with you," Amina said, and Achilles saw the sincerity in her eyes.

"Well, you can consider yourself forgiven, my lovely Amina," Achilles said, laughing, then he pulled her close.

"Wallahi, my dear Achilles, I am going to make you so happy," Amina whispered, and then she kissed Achilles with all the passion she could muster.

Overhead, a small airplane dipped its wings and flew dangerously low in the wide blue skies over the island.

"This is the Coast Guard, please hang on we're coming down," shouted a male voice over a megaphone.

Amina Al-Mahdi and Achilles Jackson could hear people shouting to get their attention, but the remarkable pair ignored them completely.

Indeed, at that moment, these two star-crossed lovebirds were very much in a world of their own.

FINDING THE WAY

"Adam, if you don't have my money, you lying little sack of shit, I'm going to get your balls," Pedro Alvarez said menacingly as he looked at the stocky, dark-skinned young Haitian man who stood before him.

283

Even though it was an unseasonably cool morning in early June, Adam Gustave had begun to sweat profusely.

Pedro's acolytes, a portly Mexican guy named Oscar and a tall, lean and tattooed Asian dude named Chan, laughed at their boss humor while eyeing Adam coldly.

Adam had just come out of Royal Barbershop, a spot where he'd been going for years, and he'd crossed the street, intent on checking out the new Indian restaurant.

After getting his hair cut, and chatting with his favorite barber, the young brother was definitely feeling good.

Unfortunately for him, the restaurant was closed. And then he got the urge to take a leak, and went behind the restaurant to do his business.

284

That's when he ran into Pedro Alvarez, leader of the local thugs, to whom he happened to owe about a thousand dollars...

"I'm sorry, Pedro, I don't have the whole thing, if you could just give me more time," Adam mumbled, and he was abruptly cut off when Pedro decked him, square in the jaw.

Adam went sprawling against the wall, and was so dizzy that Chan and Oscar had to help him up. Shaking his head, Pedro pulled out his switchblade, and held it inches from Adam's face.

"You're fucked, Adam," Pedro said nastily, and Adam looked into the Latino gangster's eyes and saw cruelty and grim determination.

Without hesitation he did the first thing that came to mind, and swung his leg at Pedro's crotch, catching him squarely in the nuts.

285

Doubling over in pain, Pedro dropped his blade, and Adam shoved his way past the stunned Chan and Oscar, and slipped away.

"Dude left me no choice," Adam said to himself as he ran across McArthur Avenue, one of Vanier's busiest streets, and made his way past a certain Asian restaurant where he'd dined a few times.

Glancing the park in the distance, he made his way there, hoping to lose his pursuers. *Go away bozos,* Adam thought.

Chancing a glance backwards, Adam saw that Pedro and company were still after him, and they were rapidly closing the gap between them and their prey.

Adam crossed the park and made his way to Donald Street, and ran as fast as he could. Earlier that day, he'd walked on Donald Street as he made his way to Soleil Des Iles, a neat little Haitian restaurant that served the best food, in spite of its ghetto location.

After eating some tasty Haitian food while chatting the cute dreadlocked and big-bottomed Haitian gal working behind the counter, Adam exited, feeling good.

The young man left the restaurant and walked to McArthur to get his haircut. That's when everything started to go wrong...

As Adam ran and ran, he came across a large building with a fence around it. Any port in a storm, Adam thought.

Beggars can't be choosers, the desperate young man thought as he made a mad dash across the building parking lot.

He saw a door that was slightly ajar and made a bee line for it, intent on hiding inside until he could call the cops or something.

Adam had no love for the guys and gals in blue, but that day, he would have kissed them if they were around to save him from Pedro and his thugs.

The Latino gangster had a bad reputation, even for a loan shark. Seriously, this nasty piece of work was cruel...

Pedro Alvarez was the new breed of gangster, the type who took no prisoners and rather than strictly working along ethnic lines, he had everyone from fellow Latinos to Asian guys and even Jamaican guys working for him.

Pedro Alvarez was one dangerous son of a bitch, rumor has it that he cut off some dude's fingers for making a pass at his girlfriend Rosita one night at a club downtown.

Adam wouldn't have gone to him unless he was truly desperate. Ever since he split from Sarah Sloane, the young White chick he'd been dating/living with, Adam had fallen on hard times.

Sarah moved out and in a desperate attempt to hang onto their Barrhaven apartment, Adam took out a loan which he couldn't repay on time.

Which led to Adam's bad deal with the loan shark. Anxious to evade his pursuers, Adam grabbed the door and went inside, and promptly shut the door behind him.

"What are you doing here, brother ? This is the sisters' entrance," came a feminine voice, and Adam Gustave nearly jumped out of his skin.

Whirling around, he found himself facing a most unexpected presence. Upon discovering who had addressed him, Adam fell silent.

The lady standing before him was tall and curvy, with light bronze skin and almond-shaped brown eyes that looked him up and down.

Clad in a Hijab, long-sleeved Black shirt and long dark blue dress, she was the picture of Islamic feminine modesty. And probably about to blow his damn cover...

"Um, sorry, ma'am, please don't be alarmed, I just want to make a phone call, I'm in trouble," Adam said quickly, and the young Muslim woman looked at him.

Before she could reply, however, there was a knock against the door. Adam looked at her pleadingly, then he looked at the door.

As the young woman headed for the door, Adam retreated into a corner. Balling his fists, he looked at the ceiling and silently prayed that this wasn't the end of his days.

Adam hadn't been anywhere near a church in ages but dammit, he was starting to wish he hadn't stopped going...

"As Salam Alaikum, brothers, I am Sister Sawsan, this is the Sisters entrance, not the Men's entrance," the young Arab woman said politely, and Adam's heart skipped a beat.

From his darkened corner, Adam could see Pedro and his acolytes at the door, speaking to the young Muslim woman.

If she was going to rat him out, Adam was a dead man walking. He'd gotten lucky earlier but there was no way he'd get past Pedro and his cronies again…

"Hello, lady, we're looking for a friend of ours, a Black dude about this high, kind of chubby, have you seen anyone like that hanging around ?" Pedro asked, and Adam held his breath as the young woman replied to the thug leader's inquiry.

Closing his eyes hard, Adam started praying to a deity he'd long stopped worshipping for deliverance in this his darkest hour. *Just give me another chance Lord*, he thought grimly.

"Brother, this is the sisters entrance of the Masjid, no man is permitted to enter here while prayer is going on," the young Muslim woman, Sister Sawsan, replied earnestly.

Adam's eyes snapped open upon hearing what she'd just said. She hadn't ratted him out. Will wonders never cease ?

Frozen with fear in his darkened corner, Adam listened to the back and forth between Sawsan and Pedro.

Finally, the young Arab Muslim woman wished the thuggish trio a good day, and then she closed the door.

"Thank you," Adam whispered, and Sister Sawsan looked at him and shook her head. Disapproval rolled off the tall, pretty, Hijab-wearing Muslim gal in waves, and Adam swallowed hard.

For the second time in less than an hour, someone was giving him the stink eye. Adam swallowed hard and sighed, and then looked at Sister Sawsan.

This young woman had just saved his ass, and Adam figured that the least he could do was explain himself...

"Who are you and why were these men after you?" Sister Sawsan asked, hands on her hips, and Adam bit his lip, and then did something he hadn't done too often in the nearly three decades he'd been living upon this earth.

He looked at a person and did not lie through his teeth. It took some effort, of course, but somehow, he managed to get through it...

"Well, sister, my name is Adam, and those thugs, Alvarez and his buddies, they're after me because I borrowed money from them," Adam Gustave said earnestly, and Sister Sawsan nodded.

As a stunned Adam looked on, Sister Sawsan drew closer to him, and then, amazingly, she gently touched his face.

Adam winced, for Sister Sawsan touched him where Pedro Alvarez had struck him. It still hurt like hell...

"Well, they've really done a number on you, you shouldn't mess with such dangerous characters, Adam," Sister Sawsan said, and when she looked at him, Adam could have sworn that he saw concern in her lovely brown eyes.

Nodding at her, Adam thanked her for her help and then started toward the door. As he reached for the handle, Sister Sawsan grabbed his hand, and shook her head vigorously. Adam looked at her, honestly puzzled.

"You shouldn't leave yet, Adam, they might still be around," Sister Sawsan said, by way of explanation, and then she finally get go of Adam's hand.

Adam looked at her thoughtfully and nodded in agreement. It was true, Pedro Alvarez and his cronies might still be hanging around.

They had lost Adam's scent for now but like hunting dogs, they would eventually pick it up. Staying out of sight was probably a good idea...

"You're right, Sister Sawsan, what was I thinking ?" Adam said, and the young Muslim woman smiled at him.

Taking out his cell phone, he tried to call the police, in case Pedro Alvarez and company were really still around, and realized that his cellphone was dead.

Less than two percent on the battery. Adam tucked it back in his pocket, and looked at his unexpected savior...

"So, first time in a Masjid, I take it, Brother Adam ?" Sister Sawsan said with a sly smile, and Adam nodded, and took a look around.

Yes, Adam had never been inside a Masjid before. Sure, he knew a lot of Arab students and Somali students at his old stomping grounds, Saint Gabriel Academy.

Hell, Adam ran into a lot more of them at Carleton University during the three years he spent there, before he dropped out. Yeah, he'd seen a lot of pretty Muslim ladies.

None of them were anything like Sister Sawsan, though...the young Muslim woman was definitely something else.

297

"Yes, I'm, well, I was raised Adventist but I stopped going to church, this place kind of reminds me of some antique churches I've visited, kind of serene," Adam said thoughtfully as he took a look around.

The place was vast, with no icons and no furniture on the Oriental carpet. There were shelves full of Koran books near the front, and that was about it.

The interior of the place was very Arabian in design, reminding Adam of structures he'd seen in the series *Sinbad* when he was younger.

"So, Adam, you stopped going to church, do you still believe ?" Sister Sawsan asked, and there was a seriousness in her tone of voice and on her lovely face that gave Adam Gustave pause.

Gently he bit his lip, and searched inward for the right answer. He sensed that religion was a serious matter for Sister Sawsan, after all this chick was in a Masjid on a Saturday night, instead of working or hanging out and having fun like most young women her age.

"Sister Sawsan, I stopped going to church because a lot of people at the Haitian Adventist church in downtown Ottawa hate my guts, hell, I almost got killed today because I messed with the wrong people, and I'm alive because of you, I'd say that's a sign from the Lord," Adam said, smiling faintly.

Adam paused for effect, and Sawsan looked at him. He was brutally honest for a change, and Sister Sawsan picked up on it. A sly smile crept into her lovely face...

"Well, that's a lovely thing for you to say, Adam, now, while you're hiding from your thug pals, how about you help a sister clean up?" Sister Sawsan said, and she smirked as she handed a stunned Adam a broom.

The young man smiled, and took the broom after a slight hesitation. As Sister Sawsan walked away, to clean another part of the Masjid, Adam watched her intently, fascinated. There was something about her...

"Hmmm, looks like Muslim cutie has a really nice butt on her," Adam whispered to himself, and he smiled as he began to broom the Masjid carpet.

Adam couldn't help thinking of the last time he used a broom. He'd been living in his hometown of Cap-Haitien, northern Haiti, at his grandmother Elise Gustave's house.

His parents, Louis and Nadine Gustave sent him to the island of Haiti for the summer, to punish him for being a wild brat, and he ended up loving it in his ancestral homeland...

"Oh, and Adam ? Stop staring at my ass," Sister Sawsan called out over her shoulder, and Adam Gustave gulped in surprise.

When Sister Sawsan turned and looked at him, he smiled sheepishly and then busied himself using the broom and dust pan like his life depended on it.

Part of him wanted to slip out the Masjid door and take his chances with Pedro Alvarez and his cronies, but for some reason, he wanted to stick around. And Sister Sawsan definitely had something to do with it...

"What did I get myself into ?" Adam asked himself with a smile, and he finished helping Sister Sawsan with cleaning up the Masjid.

Afterwards, he left, but not before thanking her profusely for not ratting him out to Alvarez and his acolytes...

"Brother Adam, may I suggest you leave whatever line of work you're in ? Next time I might not be here to save your ass, now good night," Sister Sawsan said sharply as Adam looked at her sheepishly.

Having closed the Masjid doors, Sister Sawsan got in her car and drove away. No, she did not offer Adam a ride...

As Adam lay on his bed that night, he thought about the events of the day. Getting away from Alvarez and his thugs wouldn't have been possible without the miraculous intervention of Sister Sawsan.

Upon getting home, Adam looked her up on Facebook and Instagram, along with LinkedIn, of course.

According to her Facebook profile, Sawsan Ibrahim, also known as Sister Sawsan among Muslim students at the University of Ottawa, was born and raised in Al Madinah, Saudi Arabia.

Oh, and Sawsan was quite active with Muslim community activities, and a few other things including women's rights groups in the Ottawa area.

"Oh my," Adam said to himself, for Sawsan Ibrahim was lovely and quite intriguing. And if it weren't for her, he'd be either in the hospital or the morgue.

Most likely the morgue since Alvarez wasn't known to be the merciful type. A fate Adam was more than desperate to avoid.

Sawsan Ibrahim lay in bed that night, tossing and turning, unable to sleep. In a few months, she'd head back to Saudi Arabia.

With her parents, Wafa and Sultan Ibrahim deceased, and her brother Ismail having made too many enemies by getting into business dealings with the family's enemies, Sawsan knew that she'd be walking into trouble the moment she set foot on Saudi soil.

Sawsan thought of how strange life had been these past few months. After graduating from the University of Ottawa with a degree in bio-medical engineering, she thought about doing additional studies and then try to get into medical school.

Sawsan took the MCAT and then, confident in her test scores, she sent numerous applications to various schools.

The rejection letter from the University of Toronto School of Medicine dashed those hopes for the time being...

Astonished by this latest reversal, Sawsan spiraled into a mini-depression, until, after speaking with some friends, she decided to recharge her batteries...

Feeling in need of a bit of fun, Sawsan surprised herself by accepting Adam's invitation to hang out with him.

They met at the Rideau Center where they walked to Brothers SSawsanrma and grabbed a bite, then headed to the nearby *By Towne Cinema*.

"Thanks for taking me out, Adam, I needed that," Sawsan said, smiling as the two of them walked out of the theater, onto the Ottawa evening.

"Anytime, Sawsan, you saved my ass, this is the least that I can do," Adam said, smiling, and the young woman nodded.

"I just did what any true Muslim would have done, I helped a lost soul in need," Sawsan said earnestly, and Adam smiled admiringly.

"Your faith is really important to you, eh?" Adam asked, and he watched as a beautiful, eerie light came to Sawsan's eyes.

"Do you have something against my faith?" Sawsan asked, in a somewhat terse tone, and Adam quickly raised his hands.

"No ma'am, I have respect for all religions," Adam said, talking really fast, and Sawsan grinned and playfully elbowed him.

"You're so jumpy, Adam, cute but jumpy," Sawsan said, laughing, and Adam slowly exhaled the breath he hadn't even realized he'd been holding.

"Um, thanks, so, Sawsan, tell me more about you," Adam said, and the young woman smiled and licked her lips.

"Alright, I'm from Saudi Arabia, and I'm an international student, just chilling in Ottawa," Sawsan said, grinning.

"Cool, I'm of Haitian descent, I'm just working for now, and trying to stay out of trouble," Adam said with a smile, and Sawsan shot him a look.

"Adam, listen to me, you should stay away from whatever activity got you on those thugs radars," Sawsan said, cocking an eyebrow.

"Alright, Sawsan, I owed money to these guys, and I'm working to get them off my back," Adam admitted.

"Hmm, what am I going to do with you?" Sawsan said, smiling faintly, and Adam grinned and shrugged.

"I could think of a few things," Adam said, and his eyes flitted up and down Sawsan's curvy body, and the young Hijabi's eyes narrowed.

"Brother, lower your gaze," Sawsan chastised him, using the same tone that older Muslim women used to shame rambunctious young men in her homeland of Saudi Arabia.

"My bad, Sawsan, you're a very beautiful woman," Adam said, and Sawsan grinned and shook her head, amused by his candor and flirtatious banter.

"Alright, Mister, let's go for a walk on the By Ward Market," Sawsan proposed, and Adam nodded as she unexpectedly linked her arm with his.

"This right there is the most fun part of Ottawa," Adam said, as he showed her the storied areas surrounding Dalhousie Street and beyond.

"Have you brought girls on dates there ?" Sawsan asked coyly, and Adam blinked nervously, surprised by her question.

"Um, once, I took a girl there once, yeah," Adam said, and he thought of that time he went to the *Honest Lawyer* bar with Sarah Sloane, his ex-girlfriend.

"How did things pan out ?" Sawsan asked innocently, smiling like she was totally enjoying Adam's discomfort.

"Alright, her name was Sarah, and I took her to that bar over there, it was our favorite bar," Adam said.

"Cool, let's go inside," Sawsan said excitedly, and she tugged on Adam's arm, and half-dragged him to the bar.

"Um, okay," Adam said, and he looked at Sawsan like she had two heads as they walked into the bar, and she immediately went to talk to the server.

"Good evening, sir, do you have any *Alexander Keith's*?" Sawsan said with a sweet smile, and the bartender looked her up and down.

"Um, yeah, ma'am, that's alcohol," the bartender said, and he looked at Sawsan, his blue eyes locked onto her Hijab, and the young woman laughed.

"Yes, I am aware of that," Sawsan said, and the bartender smiled, shrugged, and then poured her a shot.

"You are full of surprises," Adam said, and he watched, amazed, as the Hijab-wearing young Saudi Arabian Muslim woman chugged down her beer.

"Honey, you got no idea," Sawsan said, laughing, and she wiped her mouth with the back of her hand and winked at Adam.

"Cheers to you, Sawsan, a very mysterious and beautiful woman," Adam said, and he raised his glass to her after ordering a shot of *Alexander Keith's.*

"None of us are one-dimensional, Adam, a girl who wears the Hijab has the same needs and desires and frustrations that all girls and women have," Sawsan said to Adam, a few hours later.

311

"I heartily concur, my lady," Adam said, and after one more shot, he and Sawsan exited the bar, with everyone staring at them.

"Thanks for taking me out," Sawsan said to Adam, after he put her in a *Blue Line Taxi*, gave the driver twenty bucks, and sent her on her way.

"Crazy beautiful woman," Adam said to himself, laughing and scratching his head as Sawsan's cab drove away.

"What a life I lead," Adam thought as he headed for the nearby bus station, to begin his rather long trek home.

The next morning, as he sat inside Tim Horton's before a plate of egg and cheese sandwiches, hash browns and overly sugared coffee, Adam got a call from a certain Hijabi.

"Salaam, Adam, um, this is Sawsan," came a familiar feminine voice, and Adam grinned, and then finally replied.

"Greetings, Sawsan, how are you feeling ? Had quite a night last night," Adam replied, and he barely stopped himself from laughing.

"Oh, wow, um, I wasn't myself last night, Adam, I hope I didn't do anything too embarrassing," Sawsan said quickly, and Adam smiled and shook his head.

"No worries, nothing funny happened," Adam replied quickly, anxious to assuage Sawsan's almost palpable fears.

"My roommate told me that I got home in a cab that you paid for, I thank you, and, um, I don't normally drink," Sawsan said, speaking softly.

"Yeah, you seemed stressed out and dragged me to this bar, you knocked off a few and then I sent you

313

home, like a gentleman," Adam said, truly having fun with Sawsan's predicament.

"Yes, I was stressed out, and I am sorry if I acted inappropriately," Sawsan said, and Adam counted to three, then continued.

"It's alright, Sawsan, we are none of us angels, now, let's hang out again, perhaps a safer outing like a museum," Adam proposed, and Sawsan hastily agreed.

"Yes, a museum, that sounds heavenly," Sawsan said, rather quickly, and Adam smiled, knowing he had this in the bag.

"Cool, we'll check out the National Gallery of Canada, they're having a display on indigenous art," Adam said softly.

"Sounds good, we'll link up and go," Sawsan said, and she and Adam exchanged pleasantries and then ended the phone call.

"Now we're getting somewhere," Adam said to himself as he got ready for a job interview with the *Loblaw's* in Barrhaven.

Over the next few weeks, Adam Gustave and Sawsan Ibrahim became virtually inseparable. That trip to the museum was fun, but it was the tip of the iceberg...

"So, how do you like honest work?" Sawsan asked Adam as she visited him at Loblaw's during his lunch hour.

Working from two o'clock in the afternoon until the store closed at nine meant that Adam had a particular lousy shift.

The store hired Adam to be their cart guy, basically the guy bringing stray carts back into the store, since customers were always abandoning them in the parking lot.

After working for several hours, Adam was thrilled to get a break, especially when a surprise visitor brought him unexpected delight...

The young woman was visiting the Barrhaven Masjid, also known as SNMC, and dropped by to chat up her favorite Haitian...

"You're enjoying this, aren't you ?" Adam asked, and Sawsan grinned and tugged on his green apron, and drew closer to him.

"It's a rather nice look on you," Sawsan said softly, and suddenly her lovely face was inches from Adam's.

"Why thank you," Adam said, and he hesitated, and then went ahead and did what he'd been aching to do for ages.

Pulling Sawsan into his arms, Adam planted a kiss on the young woman's succulent-looking lips, and she kissed him back.

"Hmm, you've got sweet lips, Adam, now, what took you so long?" Sawsan replied, a sly look in her lovely brown eyes.

"We're going to get along just fine," Adam said, and Sawsan held tightly onto him, and flicked her tongue over his earlobe.

"Got some time to kill?" Sawsan said, and when Adam looked into her eyes, the passion and intensity he saw in there stunned him.

"Do I ever," Adam replied, and Sawsan giggled as he took her hand, and led her away, into the darkness of the parking lot.

Located near Marketplace Station in Barrhaven, Loblaw's is sandwiched between a bunch of stores, and is within walking distance of the Odeon movie theater, SSawsanrma Heaven restaurant, and not far from the woods behind Saint Joseph...

"We've got all the privacy we need," Adam said to Sawsan as he kissed her passionately, in a secluded area behind a copse of trees, not far from Saint Joseph.

"Indeed we do," Sawsan said, and she smiled nervously, and removed her top, tossing the stylish, long-sleeved White shirt on the grass.

"Oh my," Adam said, and he gently caressed Sawsan's breasts, astonished by her loveliness, and the young woman grinned.

"So, Mr. Gustave, do you like what you see?" Sawsan whispered, and Adam nodded, and sat her on a rocky outcropping.

In the distance, the mirror of a huge caterpillar truck, a CT660 On-Highway Truck leftover by construction workers caught the last rays of sunlight in the darkened sky.

Away from prying eyes, Sawsan and Adam made love. Sitting his beloved on the rocks, Adam knelt before her.

"How do you like that?" Sawsan said, grinning at a mesmerized Adam as she hiked up her long, traditional Islamic skirt.

"Hmmm," Adam said, and his eyes remained transfixed on Sawsan's hairy pussy. Apparently, the Saudi Hijabi was a panties-optional kind of gal...

"Adam, don't just stare at my awrah, put those lips to good use," Sawsan demanded, pinching her nipples as Adam smiled and nodded dutifully.

"Yes ma'am," Adam replied and he gently spread Sawsan's thighs and inhaled her scent, then he buried his face between her legs.

"Hmm, just like that," Sawsan cooed softly, clucking her tongue as Adam slid his own tongue into her pussy, and teased her clit.

In his lifetime, Adam had been with his share of women, but none of them were anything like Sawsan, that's for damn sure.

"So frigging hot," Adam murmured, as he lathered Sawsan's pussy with his tongue, and the young
320

woman moaned softly, loving what he was doing to her.

Sawsan shuddered violently as Adam relentlessly licked, teased and probed her pussy with his tongue and fingers, and soon she found herself spiraling on the edge of ecstasy...

"You're killing me," Sawsan cried out, and Adam continued to work his magic on her, and didn't let up until she came, gushing hot girly cum all over his face.

"More where that came from," Adam said with a slick smile as Sawsan looked at him, a stunned look on her lovely face.

"I bet," Sawsan said, smiling at Adam and then they began the kisses again. Off came his shirt and he pulled down his pants to his ankles.

"What can I say? I'm happy to see you," Adam said, his voice sounding corny to his own ears as Sawsan grabbed his dick, and stroked it gently.

Adam watched, amazed, as Sawsan yanked her traditional Islamic skirt all the way down, exposing her thick round ass and sturdy, sexy legs.

"This is a quickie, Adam, so shut up and fuck me," Sawsan said sharply, and Adam got the hint and entered her with one swift thrust.

"The things I'm going to do to that ass," Adam cooed softly, caressing Sawsan's ass as she grinded against him, driving his dick deeper inside of her.

"Less talking and more fucking," Sawsan commanded, and Adam grinned and smacked her ass, causing her to yelp.

"Hmm, talk shit now," Adam teased, gripping Sawsan's hips and thrusting deeply into her pussy, loving the way it gripped his fuck stick like a tiny hand or something...

"Oh yes," Sawsan moaned, and with that, she turned around and shot Adam a look before clenching her vaginal muscles on his dick, a move that was sure to finish him off...

"Damn," Adam cried out, and he felt his knees buckle as Sawsan's pussy gripped his dick like a vise, and that's when it happened, the moment of truth...

"Yeah, Adam, *you* talk shit *now*," Sawsan teased, and she flashed Adam a wicked smile as he exploded inside of her...

"Frigging amazing," Adam said breathlessly, and Sawsan nodded, then winced as he pulled out of her.

"Oh I know, I was there," Sawsan said with a cocky grin, and with that, the young Saudi woman began getting dressed.

Adam put his clothes back on, and stood there, watching as Sawsan went from wanton, lusty sex freak to prim and proper Hijabi. *What a woman*, he thought admiringly.

"You're a unique woman," Adam said, gently stroking Sawsan's lovely face as she adjusted the pins holding her Hijab in place, and then smoothed out her robe.

"Yes I am, Adam, and don't you forget it," Sawsan said, winking at him, and then, arm in arm, the two of them returned to the Loblaw's parking lot.

"I'll see you real soon," Adam said, and he took Sawsan's face in his hands and kissed her on the lips.

324

"Yeah, soon enough, don't fall in love now," Sawsan said teasingly, and she winked at Adam before heading to Marketplace Station, where the buses awaited.

"What did I get myself into ?" Adam said to himself, smiling as he tied his apron around his waist and returned to work.

Sawsan sat on the bus, feeling almost giddy with happiness. Things worked out much better than expected during her visit to Barrhaven, that's for damn sure.

"I've got passion back in my life, Wallahi, and it's a beautiful thing," Sawsan said to herself, and she smiled as she admired the wallpaper on her iPhone, a picture of her and Adam at the movies.

In the next few months, Sawsan Ibrahim knew that she would have difficult decisions to make about the future.

Should she stay in Canada, hoping to get into medical school and perhaps build...something, with Adam Gustave ?

"Wallahi, I'll cross that bridge when I get to it," Sawsan thought, and she looked at the dark sky, and smiled.

Her life in Ottawa was far more complicated than her secluded existence back in Saudi Arabia, that's for damn sure.

Nevertheless, Sawsan had grown fond of Canada, of her life in Ottawa, of her school and the friends she made there, and more...

Indeed, most importantly of all, Sawsan had grown fond of a certain wayward Haitian whom she met

326

under absolutely ridiculous circumstances. *Choices,*
what life is all about indeed.

THE REAL HOUSEWIVES OF SAUDI ARABIA

"Ah, the glamorous life of an exile," Najma Al-
Duwaish Obaid thought to herself as she surveyed
her neighborhood.

Located in the heart of Vanier, Ontario, the two-
story red brick building overlooked the nearby park
that occupied much of Donald Street and bordered
McArthur Avenue as well.

Although the place was alright, all things
considered, it was a far cry from her old digs in
the opulent Al-Dhahab neighborhood of central
metropolitan Riyadh, that's for sure.

Not for the first time, Najma cursed the day that her philandering husband, Mohammed Obaid, met Fatima Said, unhappily married daughter of one of Saudi Arabian society's wealthiest magnates, legendary cleric and architect Hussein Said.

The two of them carried on a torrid affair, which led to their discovery and arrest by the Mutaween, the Saudi religious police.

Mohammed Obaid's family blamed Najma for his fatal indiscretions, and after some lengthy and expensive legal wrangling, they left her destitute.

"You should leave Saudi Arabia for your own good, witch, your life is forfeit," said Khadra Obaid, Najma's mother-in-law.

The old Saudi Arabian woman spat on the ground as she spoke to her daughter-in-law, whom she always despised for many reasons.

328

Not the least of which being that Najma had grown up in the City of Toronto, Ontario, and wasn't "Saudi enough" for some.

Nevertheless, Najma took the old woman's unsolicited advice, and left the Kingdom of Saudi Arabia for Ontario, Canada.

Najma's dual Saudi/Canadian citizenship proved to be a saving grace under the circumstances. Now here she was, thirty eight years old, starting over in a new country.

Just call me the Saudi Arabian Muslim version of *The Starter Wife*, Najma thought bitterly, as she recalled her fondness for that short-lived U.S. Network series starring Debra Messing.

Like her favorite character, Najma was a stoic woman rebuilding her life after the end of a relationship.

329

Living in a two-bedroom apartment in a seedy neighborhood didn't appeal to her one bit, but Najma had no choice. For now.

"So, you graduated from the University of Toronto with a bachelor's degree in psychology in 2004, what are you qualified for, as far as today's competitive workplace ?" said Vincent Templeton, in a not-so-friendly tone.

Najma sighed and looked at the stocky, bald-headed White guy working at the employment agency which she first visited a couple of weeks ago.

Glaring almost hatefully at the annoying little Canadian man, Najma resisted the urge to slap the shit out of him.

Clad in a Black leather jacket over a red turtleneck shirt, Black silk pants and knee-high Black leather boots, her raven hair tucked under her Hijab,

Najma knew that she cut a dashing figure.
Unfortunately, her charms left Templeton cold, as
evidenced by the picture of him all hugged up with
a tall Black guy while they were both holding
rainbow flags.

Najma hadn't lived in Canada in over a decade. In
that time, the country had changed a lot. Far more
than she expected.

Interracial couples seemed to be everywhere, and
gay marriage got legalized. Fascinating stuff, to be
sure, but it wasn't getting Najma anywhere.

"I'm looking for a job, any job for which I'm
qualified, you're an employment agency, aren't you
?" Najma said icily, and Templeton shot her a look
and pursed his thin lips.

For some reason, Templeton reminded Najma of one of the teachers in the old *Harry Potter* movies. And not in a good way.

So this is what my life has come down to, needing help from the dregs of the Universe, Najma silently lamented, and she forced herself to stay calm.

Najma Obaid came to the City of Ottawa, Ontario, when it became clear to her that rent in Toronto wasn't something she could afford in the long run.

After all, when all was said and done, Najma only had sixteen thousand dollars when she arrived in Canada from Riyadh, Saudi Arabia.

Her late husband's family made sure that she left the country penniless and heartbroken. They hated her that much.

Lucky for Najma, she'd begun stashing money away the day the Mutaween stormed the Obaid residence, and dragged her husband Mohammed Obaid away in handcuffs.

After a rather brief trial, Mohammed Obaid and his lover/accomplice Fatima Said were found guilty by the Criminal Court of Saudi Arabia.

Pleas for clemency were sent to King Salman of Saudi Arabia, but fell on deaf ears. The law was the law, even for the wealthiest members of Saudi Arabian society.

Adultery carried a death sentence in the Kingdom. Thusly, Mohammed Obaid and Fatima Said were summarily executed at the infamous Deera Square, a bloody corner of Riyadh were public beheadings are carried out.

Najma remembered fainting on that hot, gruesome day. On that fateful day, she resolved to leave Saudi Arabia forever.

"Frankly, Miss Obaid, I don't think it's your resume or your educational credentials that are holding you back, it's your attitude," Templeton said, and the little man's face was suddenly beet red.

Najma smiled, resisting the urge to squeeze his nose. With his short stature, and the weird cap he always wore, he reminded her of a garden gnome.

Yeah, it was true what they say about the little guys. Always insecure, and with hidden anger issues...

"My attitude is just fine, shorty," Najma said, and she looked Templeton up and down, smiled and grabbed her purse before exiting the employment office located on Catherine Street.

There was an abundance of buses going to and fro, but Najma decided to go for a walk. She desperately needed to clear her head.

334

As she walked by a nearby school, a tall, well-dressed and handsome Black gentleman looked sharply in her direction. Najma smiled politely and continued on her way.

"Najma Al-Duwaish, is that you?" the stranger called out, and Najma turned sharply and faced him. She hadn't been called by her maiden name in ages.

In Saudi Arabia, a woman's maiden name disappeared completely after marriage. They didn't have the practice of hyphenating it like they did in Western countries.

Interestingly, the tall Black man looked at her like he knew her, and Najma found that profoundly puzzling.

"Salaam, do we know each other?" Najma asked cautiously, and the man smiled and nodded. When he smiled, Najma's heart skipped a beat.

335

Memories she'd long cast aside came back, unbidden. Najma thought of her halcyon days at the University of Toronto, and one face stood out among the countless people she met there.

Nasser Mukalay, the handsome, proudly Muslim, Congolese-born star of the University of Toronto's Varsity Basketball Team in the early 2000s. Oh, and he was also her College sweetheart...

"Come on now, Najma, it's Nasser, you forgot a brother this easily?" the handsome, chocolate-hued stranger said casually.

Nasser winked and flashed Najma that fearless smile that had the power to make her melt, *once upon a time.*

Najma smiled and swiftly crossed the distance between them. Sidestepping decades of Saudi social and cultural conditioning, Najma held out her hand, and Nasser Mukalay gently shook it.

"Good to see you again, Nasser, you look amazing, how are you?" Najma said, looking him up and down.

Although he was in his late thirties, Nasser looked almost a decade younger. *Black doesn't crack*, Najma thought enviously.

Try as she might, she couldn't hold back the bloody sands of time. With a steady diet, a rigorous exercise routine and lots of creams, Najma kept herself looking good.

Nasser on the other hand looked like a man in his late twenties, when Najma knew he was a decade older. Dammit, it just wasn't fair.

"I'm fine, Najma, I didn't know you were in town," Nasser said, and Najma felt a pleasant frisson as he suddenly pulled her into an impromptu hug.

Hmmm, someone smells good, Najma thought appreciatively. Nasser smiled at her and pursed his sexy lips, and her heart skipped a beat.

Najma did not remember how they got into the nearby Greyhound station and sat down for a quick bite, nor did she care. It felt good to catch up...

"So, you're a Dad now ?" Najma said, as Nasser showed her a picture of him standing next to a light-skinned, skinny and freckle-faced, dark-haired young woman, and there was a chubby, blonde-haired White woman in the picture as well.

For some reason, Najma's heart winced when she saw Nasser next to ladies she presumed to be his wife and daughter. It bothered her, and for the life of her, Najma couldn't tell you why...

"That's my little angel, Nadia, and the blonde gal is my wife, Kirsten Bernstein," Nasser said proudly, and there was a serene look on his face.

Najma nodded and smiled, even though the name Bernstein definitely rang a bell. Where had she heard that name before ?

Najma wracked her brain for answers, and she slipped into memory lane, back to the University of Toronto, her old stomping grounds...

Najma remembered a tall, tomboyish and kind of religious White chick whom a lot of people on campus thought was gay, if not for her obsession with Black athletcs.

Back in the day, Kirsten Bernstein was awkward, gangly, and akin to a social leper. And Nasser apparently married her. How times have changed...

"Kirsten Bernstein, that chick from the Jewish/Muslim Interfaith Alliance ? Coach Lincoln Bernstein's daughter ? You married her ?" Najma exclaimed, and Nasser smiled and shrugged nonchalantly.

Smiling on the outside, Najma quietly fumed. Back in the day, she and Nasser were one hot item. The hottest couple at U of T, in fact.

A lot of people were stunned to see the tall, athletic Congolese-Canadian Muslim stud with the pampered young Saudi Arabian woman, but they nevertheless carried on a passionate relationship for years and years.

"Yeah, um, Kirsten and I got closer, after, you and I, um, split," Nasser said hesitantly, and Najma was surprised to see an almost pained look on his dark, handsome face.

Najma nodded and gently laid her hand on his, and Nasser smiled at her but said nothing for the moment.

She remembered all too well the tumultuous events of senior year at the University of Toronto. Nasser was about to graduate with his degree in business, and had declared for the NBA Draft. Many saw him as a shoo-in for his beloved Toronto Raptors...

"Nasser, my family wants me to return to Saudi Arabia," Najma said to her boo, three months before their graduation from the University of Toronto.

341

They were lying in bed, in Nasser's off-campus apartment on Carlton Street. The evening started out nicely enough.

Najma and Nasser went to see *50 First Dates* at the movie theater, and then grabbed some Chinese food before returning home. Once there, they made passionate love...

"What are you saying, Habibti?" Nasser said, and he looked at Najma, the lovely woman who lay naked in his arms.

Earlier, they'd gone at it like sex was going out of style. Najma had been feeling frisky since the movie theater, and unleashed a sexual cyclone on Nasser once they got home.

Kissing him passionately while grabbing his crotch, Najma unzipped Nasser's pants and freed his manhood.

342

Out came his long and thick dick, which glistened in her hand as she lovingly stroked it...it looked yummy.

"Hmm, I love your stick," Najma said, smiling at Nasser as she got on her knees and proceeded to worship at his altar, as they say.

Nasser leaned against the bedroom wall as Najma took him into her mouth. From the moment Nasser first laid eyes on Najma, he knew that she was trouble.

At five-foot-ten, Najma stood taller than most Saudi women, and with her curvaceous figure, thick ass and wide hips, she drew Nasser like a moth to the flame.

And he wasn't the type to back down from a challenge. To Nasser, a woman is a woman, no matter what race or culture she hailed from.

343

If you play your cards right and she's feeling you, then she's in. Otherwise, you're not. Truly, it's simple as that.

"Hmm, do tell," Nasser whispered, and Najma winked at him as she sucked his dick and caressed his balls.

For the average Black man, Arab women were usually an unapproachable lot, but Nasser wasn't the average Black man.

And it wasn't just because of his height of six-foot-five or his movie star good looks, either. Nasser Mukalay of Congo was destined for greatness...

Born in the City of Kinshasa, Congo, to a wealthy family, Nasser came to Ontario, Canada, for University studies, and ended up taking the University of Toronto by storm as a star athlete.

Campus girls threw themselves at his feet, but the tall, handsome young Congolese brother liked a challenge.

Hence why he went after Najma Al-Duwaish, the unattainable Saudi Arabian heiress, and seduced her.

"Dick me down," Najma moaned, after polishing Nasser's dick and balls with her knowing, silky tongue.

The brother put her on all fours and smacked her big bronze butt as he ate her pussy from behind. Najma squealed in sheer delight as Nasser fingered her butt hole while he ate her pussy.

Najma was hornier than ever and ached to have him inside of her. Like the frigging teaser he was, Nasser made her wait...

345

"Ask and you shall receive," Nasser laughed, and he smacked Najma's ass, making it jiggle as he rolled a condom on his dick.

Without further ado, Nasser pushed his long, dark dick into Najma's pussy. The young Saudi woman sighed happily as Nasser's dick filled her womanhood.

Just like that, Nasser gritted his teeth as he gripped Najma's wide hips and began fucking her with swift, deep strokes.

Groaning sharply, Najma cried out as Nasser slammed his dick into her and began to fuck her silly, his absolute specialty...

"Hmm, that was nice," Najma said, taking a drag on her cigarette as she lay next to Nasser. The handsome young Congolese wrapped his arms around her and smiled.

346

Looking at him, Najma sighed happily. Tall, dark and handsome, Nasser was one hell of a guy. Born into a family of wealthy Congolese politicians and businesspeople, he nevertheless made his mark on his own in Canada.

After enrolling at the University of Toronto, Nasser applied for financial aid like everyone else, and his athletic talents earned him a spot on the basketball team. And the rest was history...

"It could be like this, just like this, forever, you know ? Just you and me, Najma," Nasser said, and he smiled at her and gently kissed her forehead.

Najma smiled sadly, and then took a deep breath. As much as Najma loved Nasser, she was not oblivious to reality.

Her family was pressuring her to return to Saudi Arabia, lest they cut her off. Najma wasn't sure how to break the news to Nasser.

Biting her lip, Najma took another deep breath, then did what she knew she had to do, even though she hated it.

"Nasser, I love you, but like I told you before, I have my world to get back to, and my responsibilities, after we graduate, I'm going to have to go back to Riyadh," Najma said, and Nasser looked at her, a hurt look on his face.

"Even after all we've been through together, all the ways you've been changed by your life in Canada, you still want to go back there?" Nasser asked, incredulous, and Najma lowered her gaze.

Nasser felt betrayed, and Najma shook her head and lowered her eyes. Try as she might, Najma couldn't make Nasser see reason.

That night, Nasser stormed out of his own apartment. With tears in her eyes, a heartbroken Najma returned to her place.

"Kirsten was there for me after you left, and we became closer friends and eventually fell in love, she's a proud Jew but her family had no qualms about letting her marry a Muslim like me, once they got to know me," Nasser said proudly, and Najma blinked, as his deep, sonorous voice snatched her out of her little trip down memory lane. Nasser was going on and on, and Najma knew she had other places to be. The moment had passed, in more ways than one...

"Nasser, I'm glad you found happiness, you're a wonderful man, I'm happy for you and Kirsten and your daughter, I hope to find my happiness someday," Najma said, and she smiled at Nasser and gently touched his face.

It was a soft and friendly gesture. Something she used to do when they were together. Nasser looked at her, astonished by her simple gesture, then he smiled and nodded.

"Good to see you again, Najma, welcome back to Ottawa, I wish you the best," Nasser said, and then he pulled something out of his pocket.

His work ID, which displayed his picture, his full name, and the letters CBSA. *So he works for the government,* Najma thought admiringly.

Nasser stood up, and held out his hand, and Najma shook it without hesitation. The two of them exchanged a smile, and then Nasser looked at her one last time before walking away.

Still got the cutest ass, that man, Najma thought with a reminiscent smile. Nasser was still one hell of a guy.

Najma gathered her belongings and walked to downtown Ottawa. It was the end of June, and the city was bustling as usual.

Once at the core, Najma walked through the Rideau Shopping Center, intent on going to the lower level to catch the 9 bus which passed by her place on Donald Street.

As she walked through the super busy shopping center, Najma saw a man asking for directions. He was tall, well-dressed, in his thirties, and Black as midnight.

"Salaam, sister, do you know where I can catch the bus to Vanier? I'm from Montreal and I've got a meeting with the RCMP in an hour," the handsome stranger said, as Najma stopped to help him out.

It was after all the Muslim thing to do. After all. Najma recalled her early days in Ottawa, and how confused she'd been since her return from Saudi Arabia.

The man, who looked like he might be from Senegal, or perhaps South Sudan, due to his extremely dark skin and ruggedly handsome features, smiled gratefully at her.

Around his neck hung a lanyard displaying a federal workers badge with the name Ahmad Taha, next to the letters G.R.C.

"Salaam, Brother Taha, I'm Najma, I'm going to Vanier myself, please, follow me," Najma said with a smile, and the tall, dark and handsome South Sudanese brother returned her smile.

"Shukran, thank you sister," Ahmad Taha said, and dutifully he followed Najma to the escalator, and they made their way to the lower levels of the Rideau Shopping Center before exiting.

Once they hit the street, Najma saw the 9 bus pull in and made a mad dash for it. Ahmad Taha easily bypassed her due to his longer legs, and held the door for her like a gentleman.

"Shukran, thanks for your help," Ahmad Taha said to Najma as he chivalrously waited for her to finish swiping her Presto Card against the bus's reader machine, and then he dropped four loonies inside, and picked up the transfer ticket.

Najma smiled at him and bade for him to sit next to her. Ahmad Taha did as Najma said, and held tightly onto his briefcase full of legal documents.

"Welcome to Ottawa, brother, it's a hectic place but us Muslims got to stick together," Najma said cheerfully, and Ahmad Taha smiled and nodded.

As the bus got on its way, the two of them bantered. It turned out that Najma's initial assessment of Ahmad Taha was correct.

The brother was indeed of Sudanese origin, though he'd been in Montreal for decades, long enough to get a degree and a cozy government job. Oh, and he was unmarried.

"Sister, you truly embody the spirit of Ramadan, thanks for your help, I'm new in town but if you ever need anything, don't hesitate to call me,"

Ahmad Taha said to a smiling Najma as he pulled out his business card.

The bus reached McArthur, and Ahmad thanked her and handed her the card. Najma smiled to herself and pocketed it, then watched Ahmad Taha as he exited.

"Salaam, brother Ahmad, see you again, Insha'Allah," Najma heard herself say, and she grinned broadly and shook her head. The Sudanese dude was something else...

This seemingly ordinary day was turning out to be much better than she initially expected. Interesting things definitely do happen from time to time.

First the encounter with Nasser, a total blast from the past, and now this rather interesting Ahmad fellow.

Cute ass on that one, and Ahmad Taha is new in town, if I get bored we might have lots of fun together, Najma thought to herself with a sly smile.

THE SAUDI MILF NEXT DOOR

"As Salam Alaikum, Miss Al-Sabhan, is Ahmed home ?" Mohamed Hersi asked, as he stood at the door of the Al-Sabhan household.

Fahima Al-Sabhan, the Riyadh-born, recently widowed lady of the house shook her head as she looked at the six-foot-tall, dark-skinned young East African Muslim man who stood before her.

There was a hopeful look on the brother's handsome chocolate face, and Fahima bit her lip, considering her words wisely.

356

Standing before Fahima, looking tall and handsome, Mohamed Hersi looked like one of the African princes of old brought back to life.

The young Somali who lived six blocks away had been good friends with her son Ahmed Al-Sabhan for ages, looked strong and confident.

Oh my, it seems that while I stopped looking, Mohamed Hersi has become quite a man, Fahima thought admiringly.

Fahima smiled at Mohamed Hersi, who blinked nervously. She'd known him for ages. Yet the Somali brother always greeted Fahima Al-Sabhan the same way.

Super formal, like a proper Muslim brother. *If only my son Ahmed were more like you*, Fahima Al-Sabhan silently lamented.

357

She'd grown so damn tired of bailing her wayward, magnet-for-trouble son Ahmed out of various jams it wasn't even funny...

"Walaikum Salaam, Brother Mohamed, Ahmed has gone to Alberta to spend a few days with his cousin Ali," Fahima Al-Sabhan replied, and Mohamed Hersi looked crestfallen.

At the age of nineteen, Mohamed Hersi still didn't have a cell phone. He studied at the University of Ottawa and worked hard at the local Loblaw's.

Mohamed was studious and hard-working, so unlike her son Ahmed, who smoked, drank, and liked to party with Western girls.

Moved by Mohamed's disappointment, Fahima Al-Sabhan invited him inside. She was off that day and could actually use some company...

"No, you won't impose, Mohamed, please, come inside and drink some tea with me, keep an old woman company," Fahima Al-Sabhan said, and Mohamed Hersi, like the prim and proper Muslim brother that he was raised to be, dared not refuse.

Fahima Al-Sabhan sat Mohamed Hersi down in her family living room, and the young man waited while she went to get some tea.

"Thank you ma'am," Mohamed Hersi said, and Fahima Al-Sabhan turned and smiled at him, and then busied herself getting the tea ready.

Fahima hummed to herself as she made tea, and briefly turned around, and caught Mohamed Hersi glancing at her.

Fahima smiled to herself, completely unsurprised by Mohamed's behavior. Truth be told, the brother had been stealing surreptitious glances her way for quite some time, every time he visited Ahmed, in fact, and Fahima Al-Sabhan found it flattering.

At the age of fifty two, Fahima Al-Sabhan was widowed, and her life had become boring and monotonous.

Ever since her husband Fahd Al-Sabhan died of a heart attack while working construction at the Shaw Center in downtown Ottawa, life hadn't been the same for Fahima.

She was lonely, and filled with grief, and found herself smothered by the sympathy and pity that she received from family and friends.

To make things worse for Fahima, the men in the Arab Muslim community of Ottawa now behaved as though she were a leper.

In the Arab world, widows are objects of pity. It didn't matter to those Arab Canadian Muslim men that Fahima Al-Sabhan was quite a catch.

Fahima had an Accounting Degree from Carleton University and worked for the Canada Revenue Agency as an auditor, and she owned her own home.

Nope, to those Arab guys, Fahima had suddenly become less than they because her husband was dead.

Yes I am sexless and lonely but not dead yet, Fahima Al-Sabhan thought bitterly. The idea that she was no longer a hot commodity bothered her...

On top of everything else, Fahima Al-Sabhan had her hands full with her troublesome twenty-year-old son Ahmed.

361

At first, he was going to Algonquin College, and planned on working in the construction field just like his late father.

And then Ahmed changed his mind, dropped out of school, and spent his days drinking, fighting and sleeping around.

The young Saudi-Canadian drunkard had gotten arrested time and again, and Fahima Al-Sabhan got absolutely sick of Ahmed's antics.

When Ahmed Al-Sabhan decided to move to the City of Edmonton, Alberta, to work in the oil sands and be free of his nagging mother, Fahima Al-Sabhan was secretly relieved.

More than once Fahima thought of Ahmed's best friend Mohamed Hersi. Back in the day, Fahima was close friends with Amal and Yusuf Hersi, Mohamed's parents.

When Fahima and Fahd Al-Sabhan moved to the City of Ottawa, Ontario, from their hometown of Beirut, Lebanon, they were one of a few Muslim families in the east end and the Hersi clan were among their first friends.

The hard-working Somali Canadian Muslim couple lived on Donald Street, one of the most storied areas in the east end of Ottawa.

Indeed, they were just a ten-minute walk from Fahima Al-Sabhan's house on quiet old Coventry Street.

Fahima Al-Sabhan envied the Hersi family, whose sons Mohamed and Idris were at the University of Ottawa, working hard and leading productive lives.

Mohamed has certainly grown into a handsome and fine young man, Fahima Al-Sabhan thought to herself as she glanced at him while putting the tea on a nice tray.

"Here you go, Mohamed, Somali-style tea," Fahima Al-Sabhan said with a smile as she set the tray on the table, and Mohamed smiled and thanked her profusely.

Fahima hadn't been prepared to receive visitors and wore gray sweatpants and an old blue sweatshirt, her long Black hair flowing freely on her shoulders.

Once upon a time, Fahima never went anywhere without her Hijab on, but those days were over. Canada had indeed changed Fahima, and she was okay with that.

"Thank you for the tea and the reception, ma'am," Mohamed Hersi said nervously, and Fahima Al-Sabhan nodded, aware of how nervous she made him.

364

When the timer on the stove rang, Fahima excused herself and went to check on the turkey she'd been cooking.

Dropping a spoon on the floor, Fahima bent to pick it up, and while turning around, she saw Mohamed looking at her with a very intense look on his handsome face.

The brother from Somalia really likes my big ass, Fahima thought with a sly smile, pleased by what she saw in Mohamed's gaze.

"Mohamed, so, tell me, how is University treating you ? Do you have a girlfriend yet ?" Fahima asked, and Mohamed Hersi shifted in his seat, suddenly looking very uncomfortable.

Fahima leaned forward, sensing the young Somali man's distress. Sighing deeply, she gently laid her hand on his lap, and Mohamed's eyes followed her

365

every move. Mohamed licked his lips, and then forced himself to speak his mind...

"Ma'am, I don't quite know how to say this, but the girls at my school don't do it for me, sometimes I wonder if I might be queer or something, the one female I liked will forever be out of my reach, so maybe the Universe is telling me something," Mohamed Hersi said, and he looked at Fahima Al-Sabhan, and shrugged.

There was a look of absolute sadness on his handsome face. Fahima's heart skipped a beat, and she fixed her gaze on Mohamed, considering his words.

"Mohamed, do not despair, you are a very handsome young man, just because a lot of girls don't do it for you doesn't mean you are gay, instead of doing this haram thing, and having sex

366

with other men, focus on the female you mention," Fahima Al-Sabhan said hopefully.

After living in the City of Ottawa for almost two decades, Fahima had grown used to seeing men kissing men and women kissing women.

Still, the thought of a handsome Muslim brother like Mohamed Hersi going that way filled her with anger...

"Mrs. Al-Sabhan, I'm sorry but you're the female who haunts my dreams, I can't have you and the girls at school don't do it for me, I think I'm doomed to be gay, sometimes I get aroused in the men's locker room," Mohamed Hersi said sadly.

That's when the young Somali man sobbed and hid his face in his hands. Fahima Al-Sabhan nodded, and gently touched the top of Mohamed's head.

The young man looked up at her, his soulful brown eyes looking very moist all of a sudden...and she held her breath.

"Habibi, do not despair," Fahima Al-Sabhan said, and with that, she took Mohamed Hersi's handsome face into her hands and looked into his eyes.

Fahima held her breath, for there was an intensity and vulnerability oozing out of Mohamed, while raw desire coursed through her core.

Fahima Al-Sabhan hadn't been with a man in the eighteen months since her husband Fahd Al-Sabhan died, and lately, sex was all that she had on her mind. And she had no way to satisfy her needs...

"Mohamed, I know what you need," Fahima Al-Sabhan whispered, and then, over his objections, she kissed him passionately.

After a brief hesitation, Mohamed Hersi wrapped his arms around Fahima Al-Sabhan, mother of his best friend Ahmed Al-Sabhan, and kissed her back.

Woman and man, beyond the boundaries of race, religion, culture, and age, tumbled on the carpeted floor, and began making love.

"You are so beautiful," Mohamed said, and a smiling Fahima Al-Sabhan nodded and then she swiftly straddled him.

Reassured as she felt him harden under her, Fahima proceeded to take off her shirt, revealing her curvaceous loveliness to a mesmerized Mohamed.

Fahima unzipped Mohamed's pants, freeing his long and thick, hard dick. Smiling, Fahima stroked Mohamed's dick and the young Somali man sighed happily.

369

"See, Mohamed ? You're hard for me because you're a man who likes women, you're not gay," Fahima Al-Sabhan said, and as a smiling Mohamed looked on, she leaned over and took his dick into her mouth.

Mohamed sighed happily as Fahima began sucking his dick, and she massaged his ball sac while fellating him.

The foxy Saudi Canadian MILF got him harder than a rock in no time, and when Fahima finally stopped, tugging on his hard dick, Mohamed thanked his lucky stars.

"You're so beautiful, Fahima, I want to taste you," Mohamed said in a breathless voice, and Fahima Al-Sabhan hesitated, then smiled.

Truth be told, Fahima was surprised at her own actions. She'd definitely crossed the line by grabbing Mohamed Hersi and sucking his dick.

Good Saudi housewives don't grab young Black men and suck their dicks, Fahima chastised herself, and then her pussy twitched when Mohamed took off his shirt, revealing his washboard abs.

Almost dreamily Fahima touched Mohamed's chest and abs, which were astounding, and looked into his eyes, hungrily.

"Come taste me then, Mohamed, I haven't been with a man since my Fahd died, be gentle with me," Fahima Al-Sabhan said as she lay back on the carpet, resting her head against some pillows she'd snatched from the couch.

Mohamed nodded, and smiled as Fahima spread her thick, golden thighs invitingly, revealing her hairy

371

pussy. As he brought his face closer, he inhaled Fahima's scent, and then went to work on her.

"Oh my, Fahima, you smell and taste wonderful," Mohamed Hersi paused to say, and then he buried his face between Fahima's thighs, and began feasting on her pussy.

Fahima closed her eyes and licked her lips, finally relaxing and enjoying herself as Mohamed went to work on her.

As Mohamed licked her clit and fingered her pussy, Fahima exhaled sharply. She hadn't experienced such carnal delights in quite some time...

"Hmmm, don't stop," Fahima squealed, feeling a wave of sweet pleasure and wicked pain as Mohamed worked three fingers into her pussy while teasing her clit with his tongue.

The Somali brother had her right where he wanted her. Fahima was tickled pink when Mohamed switched things up on her and put her on all fours.

Mohamed let out a gasp of admiration as Fahima shook her big bronze booty for him, and she laughed out loud.

"Dammit, Fahima, I've been dreaming about that ass for ages," Mohamed blurted out, and Fahima grinned as he kissed her butt, and then began eating her pussy from behind.

After giving her pussy a tongue bath, Mohamed pressed his hard dick against Fahima's vaginal opening and then pushed his way inside.

Fahima smiled happily as Mohamed gripped her wide hips and began fucking her with swift, deep strokes.

373

Fahima hadn't had a good dicking in quite a while, and Mohamed was just what she needed to make up for lost time.

"Fuck me harder, Mohamed," Fahima Al-Sabhan squealed, and Mohamed grinned and happily obliged her, spanking the Saudi Canadian MILF's big ass as he slammed his dick into her pussy.

Fahima's screams of passion filled the air, and as her pussy gripped his dick like a vise, Mohamed cried out her name.

Mohamed fucked her with gusto, loving the way Fahima cut loose, grinding that big round ass against his groin and screaming her brains out.

He'd long dreamed of taking her like this, his best friend's sultry mama, and she was everything he could have imagined and more...

"Hmmm, I'm beat, you're amazing, Fahima,"
Mohamed said as he lay next to her, an hour or so
later.

Lying side by side on the carpet, their bodies
glistening with sweat, Fahima and Mohamed
exchanged a smile.

The curvy Saudi Arabian Muslim woman looked at
the handsome, virile young Somali stud who lay
next to her and caressed his hairy, muscular chest.

The handsome, passionate Mohamed had energy to
burn, and made Fahima feel more alive than she'd
felt in ages...

"You're amazing too, Mohamed, I can't stand the
thought of a fine dick like yours going into any
other woman, or any frigging gay man, when you
feel horny, I want you to come to me, I'm discrete

375

and fun," Fahima said, and then she kissed Mohamed on the lips, then got up.

Mohamed's eyes followed her every move as Fahima stood naked and headed to the washroom, shaking that big bronze ass from side to side like a pendulum of temptation.

"Sounds like a plan," Mohamed replied, and Fahima turned around and shot him a wink before going into the washroom.

Mohamed began putting his clothes back on, and then got ready to leave. When Fahima came back, he watched her get dressed, then gave her a peck on the lips and a hug before exiting the premises.

Mohamed Hersi felt giddy with excitement as he left the Al-Sabhan household with an extra bounce in his step.

376

The young Somali Muslim man smiled to himself as he boarded the bus and headed to downtown Ottawa.

The day turned out a lot better than Mohamed could have anticipated. Like a frigging *Letter to Penthouse*, it would seem.

Remembering Fahima's raw passion, Mohamed hummed to himself. He felt like he was walking on sunshine, as they say.

Who would have thought that his fib about sexual confusion could have landed him into bed with the fine Saudi Arabian woman he'd been fantasizing about for ages ?

Life is funny that way. Mohamed Hersi looked forward to spending more quality time with the lovely Fahima Al-Sabhan, now that this annoying loser son of hers Ahmed was finally out of the way.

THE OVERNIGHT CLEANING CREW

"The myth about all Saudi Arabian people being rich is just that, a myth, I mean, if you believe that, then explain to me how come everyone in countries like America and Canada isn't rich," Fawzia Fetieh said, somewhat tersely.

Truth be told, Fawzia was a bit peeved at having to explain such a fundamental thing to her close friend Ali Diallo.

The charming young brother had a habit of getting on her nerves, although Fawzia simply couldn't stay mad at him.

378

Irked by this rather asinine discussion, the thirty-something Saudi woman tried not to roll her eyes as she and her co-worker and good friend Ali Diallo cleaned the CRA building located on Laurier Street in downtown Ottawa.

It was after hours, and the two of them bantered as they cleaned the whole place, floor by floor. Such were their tasks as building maintenance personnel...

"Oh, I think it's because every time I meet a Saudi person, they're either an international student whose every expense is paid for by their government, or a rich businessperson, and then there are those Saudi royals who spend a million bucks while shopping in Paris in just one weekend," Ali Diallo replied, shrugging casually.

A look of amazement creased the six-foot-tall, wiry and muscular young Guinean Muslim's dark, handsome face.

"Ali, stop daydreaming," Fawzia said, smiling as she snapped her fingers mere inches from Ali Diallo's face, and the young man smiled and shrugged.

Fawzia continued to roll the cleaning cart on the seventh floor, and paused upon reaching the washrooms.

Ask any cleaner from here to the end of the world, and they'll tell you that female washrooms are usually infinitely dirtier than the male ones.

Fawzia still had terrifying nightmares about the last time she cleaned the ladies room in this particular office building...

"Alright, Fawzia, no need to faint, I'll do the ladies room, but you'll owe me," Ali said with a wink, and

Fawzia sighed in relief as he dutifully knocked on the washroom door, even though it was after hours.

No reply came, and Ali Diallo began humming a song as he pushed his car into the washroom, and began cleaning up. *What a man*, Fawzia thought, smiling in amazement.

"Hey, Ali, I'm small but I'm feisty, I just don't like going in there, Shawarma is on me next Friday after Masjid prayer," Fawzia shouted as Ali Diallo grinned and closed the washroom door behind him.

Standing five-foot-three, and weighing a hundred and thirty pounds soaking wet, Fawzia was used to having people underestimate her.

She often surprised them with her willpower and cleverness, and also her wicked sense of humor. That's how Fawzia got Ali Diallo wrapped around her little finger.

If someone told Fawzia Fetieh three years ago that she'd leave her old life in the City of Tabuk, Saudi Arabia, for an uncertain new existence in the City of Ottawa, Ontario, she would have laughed.

Born to an upper-middle-class Saudi family, and educated at Brunel University in the City of London, England, Fawzia was brought to Canada under dire circumstances.

Fawzia sought to escape the tribal conflict which pitted her family, the Fetieh Clan, against the larger and more powerful Al-Amoudi Clan.

Jafar Al-Amoudi, head of said Clan happened to have the backing of the Al-Saud family, which rules the Kingdom of Saudi Arabia.

As various men and women of the Fetieh Clan were put to the sword for their complicity in a plot against the Al-Amoudi Clan and their allies the

382

House of Saud, Fawzia was forced to flee the Kingdom of Saudi Arabia.

The execution of her father-in-law Amir Al-Fetieh had been a wake-up call for Fawzia. The fates had not been smiling upon her...

Thirty five years old at the time of the incident, on the verge of being repudiated by her philandering husband Wazir Al-Fetieh for her apparent barrenness, Fawzia was already leading a precarious life when her whole world went to hell.

"If you ever return to Saudi Arabia, you will be put to death, the blood feud between these two great houses will not end until every last member of the Fetieh Clan is dead," said Mohamed Fakir, the seedy government official who helped Fawzia Fetieh escape from Saudi Arabia.

Fawzia nodded at her benefactor and took the government documents he'd secured for her at considerable risk to his own life.

Silently Fawzia thanked her lucky stars to have a friend like Mohamed Fakir. Without his aid, she would have died in Riyadh.

"Thank you for helping me, my friend, I will not forget this," Fawzia said, and Mohamed Fakir nodded gravely, and then walked her to the King Khalid International Airport, the crown jewel of metropolitan Riyadh.

From this spot, tons of tourists, including wealthy American and European business types, arrived in the Saudi Arabian capital every day.

As Fawzia boarded the plane, she looked out the window, at her homeland. Closing her eyes hard,

Fawzia Fetieh said goodbye to the Kingdom of Saudi Arabia forever.

When Fawzia Fetieh arrived in the City of Ottawa, Ontario, she thought life would get better. After all, this was Western society.

Fawzia had never been to the Capital of Canada before but imagined it wasn't that different from London, UK, where she lived for a time while studying business management at Brunel University.

Didn't those friendly and oh-so nice Canadians maintain close ties to British society, particularly the British royals ?

Fawzia imagined that Canada was like Britain, only geographically bigger. Time would prove Fawzia dead wrong, and then some...

385

Three years after arriving in the Canadian Capital, Fawzia managed to convince an immigration judge not to send her back to Saudi Arabia.

They'd accepted her refugee claim and granted her protected person status, but her permanent residence application was still in processing.

The permanent residence card was key to Fawzia's whole future. Her entire life depended on it.

Even though Fawzia held a business degree from a British University, no Canadian institution worth her time would hire her due to her whole status-in-limbo thing. Canadian bureaucracy at its finest.

In the meantime, Fawzia worked as a cleaner in a downtown office building to pay her rent and groceries, preparing for the day when she'd get her permanent residence card and finally be able to lead a better life.

More than once, Fawzia caught herself lamenting her old life in the City of Riyadh, Capital of Saudi Arabia.

Fawzia lived in a walled villa, and had servants catering to her every whim. Now look at her life...it was definitely nothing to write home about.

"Dammit, sometimes I hate my life," Fawzia muttered to herself, as she dutifully cleaned the men's washroom.

As Fawzia cleaned the washroom, she put on her headphones, and listened to her favorite song, *Numb.*

Chester Bennington, the lead singer of the band behind that timeless song died recently, shocking the hell out of millions of fans, Fawzia Fetieh among them.

As Fawzia fell into the groove of the song, she began to do the bump and grind, like she'd seen so many young women do while out and about on the streets of Ottawa.

"Hot damn, never thought I'd live to see the day when a Saudi mama shook her big booty," Ali Diallo shouted, as he tapped Fawzia on the shoulder, nearly causing the startled woman to jump out of her skin.

Fawzia looked at Ali Diallo as though she'd seen a ghost, and fright gave way to anger as the tall, dark-skinned and handsome young Guinean Muslim stood there, laughing merrily at her.

"Ali, wipe that smirk off your face or I'll slap you," Fawzia said, shaking her head and trying not to

388

laugh as Ali Diallo stood there, hands on his hips, a smug smile on his face.

Fawzia had known Ali for some time, and grown used to his antics. The brother hailed from the Faranah region of the Republic of Guinea, and had been living in Ottawa for the past two years.

Like Fawzia, Ali Diallo applied for permanent resident status. He came to Canada for school and work, and also to escape political strife back home.

The Canadian government had yet to answer his request, and in the meantime, Ali Diallo worked as a cleaner while taking classes at Algonquin College.

"Fawzia, my dear, I must warn you, when I meet a slap-happy, big-booty women, I tend to date them," Ali Diallo said, and Fawzia rolled her eyes.

After knowing each other for some time, she and Ali sometimes hung out outside of work, and she'd seen the long list of big-booty women, usually Black or Hispanic, whom he tended to date.

Floozies, the whole lot of them. Fawzia sometimes wondered why a good Muslim like Ali Diallo flocked to such women, instead of getting a pious, Hijab-wearing Muslim sister...

"Ali Diallo, my dearest friend, if you had me, you wouldn't know what to do with me," Fawzia replied, and she stepped closer to him, totally getting into his personal space, as they say.

Ali Diallo grinned nervously, in the manner of young men the world over when a feisty woman called their bluff.

Fawzia grinned, totally savoring the moment. Ali Diallo was usually so damn cocksure, so full of himself.

There she was, her face inches from his, and he looked more nervous than a cat in a room full of barking dogs...

"Or I could do this," Ali Diallo said, and a stunned Fawzia blinked in surprise as the young Guinean pulled her close, and then kissed her.

If lightning had struck Fawzia right then and there, it wouldn't have shocked her more. Fawzia was surprised, yes, but then she surprised herself, and Ali, by kissing him back.

As the young man held her close and caressed her while sliding his tongue down her throat, Fawzia felt tingles of pleasure cascading through her curvaceous yet long-neglected body.

"Hmm, you have sweet lips, Mr. Diallo," Fawzia said, smiling up at him, and Ali Diallo grinned and nodded.

Ali Diallo was still grinning when Fawzia grabbed his ass and gave it a firm squeeze. Something she'd been wanting to do for ages.

Ali Diallo smiled and kissed Fawzia again. Without any thought to where they were, or consequences of any kind, they began making love.

"You're so beautiful," Ali Diallo said, as he hoisted Fawzia up on the washroom counter, and the curvy, bronze-skinned and brown-eyed beauty winked at him.

Fawzia licked her lips as Ali Diallo stroked her lovely face affectionately, and then caressed her breasts.

Clad in a long-sleeved dark blue shirt featuring the words "It's Trudeau" and faded blue jeans, her long curly dark hair hidden by a modest ebony Hijab,

Fawzia definitely hadn't come ready for a seduction, but who cares ?

"Shukran, go for it handsome," Fawzia replied, and she giggled as Ali Diallo kissed her hand, and then his hands began roaming all over her curvy body.

Emboldened, Fawzia took off her shirt, and Ali smiled and caressed her breasts as she unclasped her bra.

Gently he pressed his lips against her nipples and sucked on them. Fawzia leaned back against the mirrored wall, and sighed happily as Ali began pleasuring her. It had indeed been too long since she'd known a man's touch...

"The things I'm going to do to you," Ali Diallo whispered, looking into Fawzia's eyes as he pulled down her pants, and he smiled upon noticing her bright pink panties.

393

Fawzia smiled and pulled them down, exposing her hairy pussy. Ali knelt before her and brought his dark, handsome face to her crotch.

Fawzia spread her thick bronze thighs invitingly, and Ali Diallo inhaled her scent, and then buried his face between her legs.

Fawzia licked her lips and smiled as Ali began eating her pussy. She was pleasantly surprised that the younger man knew what he was doing as he teased her clit with his tongue, and began fingering her pussy...

"Hmm, Ali, please don't stop," Fawzia cooed softly, and she caressed the back of Ali's head as he licked her pussy.

Soon the brother from Guinea had her tingling all over, and then some. Fawzia squirmed on the washroom counter, overwhelmed with sensations as Ali pleasured her.

Fawzia screamed with wild abandon as she came, violently orgasmic for the first time in what seemed like ages.

When Fawzia calmed down, somewhat, she looked at Ali, amazed at such prowess from such a young man.

"Guess I revved up your engine, mama," Ali Diallo said with a cocky smile, and Fawzia grinned and shook her head.

As passionate as Ali was, he still sounded like a young pup, but that didn't stop Fawzia from appreciating his charm.

Grabbing the young Guinean Muslim stud by the collar and kissed him. Unzipping Ali's pants, Fawzia freed his dick, and began stroking it at once.

"Ali, sometimes in life you need to shut up and relax," Fawzia said, and Ali Diallo nodded as she pumped her hand up and down his shaft.

The Saudi gal smiled, pleased that her lover got the message. They switched things around, and Ali leaned against the wall as Fawzia knelt before him and took his dick into her mouth.

Fawzia took her sweet time as she pleasured Ali, and when he came, she tasted a bit of his cum, and let the rest fall to the floor.

"Let's do this," Ali said, and Fawzia nodded, and watched as he pulled a condom out of his wallet, unwrapped it and rolled it on his dick.

Fawzia licked her lips and turned around, resting her arms against the washroom counter. Admiring their reflections in the mirror, Fawzia watched as Ali came up behind her.

396

The young Guinean had a mesmerized look on his handsome face as he watched her big bronze butt shake from side to side.

Fawzia smiled and thrust her big round butt out, and Ali Diallo gently caressed it, and slapped it playfully.

"Shut up and fuck me," Fawzia said, and Ali was happy to oblige. Gripping Fawzia's hips, Ali pushed his dick into her pussy and began to fuck her with gusto.

Fawzia licked her lips appreciatively as Ali fucked her with gusto, pounding her pussy with deep, powerful thrusts.

Fawzia's screams soon filled the room, and she cut loose, giving back as good as she got, grinding her ass against Ali's groin as he fucked her.

Hard and fast Ali pounded away at Fawzia, and his grunts of effort mingled with her pleasure-filled moans.

"Now that's what I call a much-needed break," Ali Diallo said, a few minutes later, as he and Fawzia readjusted their clothes.

Fawzia looked at the handsome brother who'd just fucked the hell out of her and grinned. Ali Diallo was full of surprises.

Although his manly rod left Fawzia pleasurably sore down below, Ali had much to learn, about women and life in general.

Lucky for him, Fawzia didn't mind teaching him a thing or two. With a little coaching, he could become so much more...

"Yeah, stop grinning like a psycho and clean that up, handsome, we got another floor to do," Fawzia said, in that bossy tone of hers.

Raising an eyebrow, Fawzia pointed downward, indicating the mess Ali Diallo left on the floor after he came, thanks to her stunning oral skills.

"Fawzia, if you keep bossing me around, I'll smash that big Saudi ass of yours even harder next time," Ali Diallo said with a grin.

Upon hearing those words, Fawzia's heart skipped a beat, and her pussy twitched. *The brother has quite an effect on me*, she thought.

Unblinking, the young Guinean Muslim looked at Fawzia, and she turned around and smiled, then shook her ass at him while readjusting her Hijab.

Without another word, Fawzia Fetieh winked at Ali and left the washroom. Ali Diallo smiled to himself, shook his head in amazement and went back to work.

FEMALE DOMINATION IN TODAY'S SAUDI ARABIA

The Kingdom of Saudi Arabia is thought of by many as a forbidden place. To the billion plus men and women around the planet Earth who call themselves Muslims, Saudi Arabia is the Heartland of Islam.

To Western feminists, Saudi Arabia is a backwards land and a veritable prison for the female sex.

To the African, Filipino and Indian workers who come to Saudi Arabia for labor and end up mistreated by their Saudi Arabian employers, the

400

Kingdom is a place to avoid. Still, what is life like for the women of Saudi Arabia ?

Take a look at a young Saudi Arabian Muslim woman's life before passing judgement on her or her countrymen, please and thank you.

Lots of people who have never been to Saudi Arabia are quick to judge, and in doing so, they oversimplify an entire nation.

They forget that Saudi Arabian women are, first of all, women, and any man who tries to make a woman do what she does not want to do does so at his own peril...

The lady in question is a newlywed from a privileged background, one who is having a tough time adjusting to life as the wife of a mercurial younger man.

401

Sadiya Al-Harbi is twenty nine years old, and is newly married to Muhammad Al-Saud, the son of a wealthy Saudi Arabian family.

The fact that Muhammad is five years younger than his wife was seen as odd by both of their families, but the pair nevertheless got married, one fine day in the City of Dammam, in the Eastern Province of Saudi Arabia.

Many in the City of Dammam thought of Muhammad Al-Saud and Sadiya Al-Harbi as an odd match.

After all, Muhammad Al-Saud hadn't been the same since he went to study civil engineering at the University of California in the City of Los Angeles.

While at UCLA, Muhammad Al-Saud explored a brand new world. Young, wealthy, and eager to experiment, Muhammad indulged in wine, clubbing, and lots of women of course.

Along the way, the young man also discovered a penchant for certain 'odd' sexual practices, to say the least.

Sadiya Al-Harbi is a classy young Saudi Arabian Muslim woman. The daughter of Imam Rafiq Al-Harbi, one of the most prominent clerics in all of Saudi Arabia, Sadiya was raised to be a pious Muslim woman.

Life wasn't easy for Sadiya, whose mother Amina Abugabal was a Black Muslim woman from Sudan who married a Saudi Arabian Muslim preacher.

403

Growing up to be a six-foot-tall, curvy, biracial woman in the Heartland of Islam taught Sadiya to be brave in the face of adversity.

In the Kingdom of Saudi Arabia, a land where more than fifteen percent of the population has some African heritage, the bias against Black folks remains strong in the heart of the Arabs.

Casual racism was pretty much a fact of life for non-Arabs living inside the Kingdom of Saudi Arabia.

Sadiya's father tried to marry her off for a while, but only Muhammad the reformed party guy who spent years living in the United States of America showed any interest in Sadiya.

Other suitors found Sadiya's mixed blood 'tainted, and didn't want her to produce offspring that would alter their pristine lineage.

At the time that Muhammad Al-Saud and his parents approached Sadiya's father to ask for her hand in marriage, the young woman was dangerously close to thirty.

Her father the Imam was relieved to marry her off. After the wedding, Sadiya found her husband Muhammad's ways strange, but dismissed them as leftover Western nonsense from his days spent in the United Snakes of America.

All was well, until the day Sadiya and her husband had an argument over her lavish spending, and he came after her. Her reaction surprised them both...

405

"Hmm, you have some fire, I see, nice, I am definitely more into you now," Muhammad Saud said, rubbing his cheek with his hand and smiling at Sadiya Al-Harbi, the obedient Saudi Muslim housewife who stunned him.

Indeed, Sadiya just slapped the shit out of him after Muhammad cornered her, berated her and then pointed his index finger at her face.

Sadiya, who stood there, breathing heavily, looked at her husband through angry brown eyes, and she pursed her lips before speaking.

"Husband, I am a good wife and swore to honor and obey you in all things but do not come at me this way," Sadiya said, her tall, curvy body trembling, and Muhammad grinned nastily, growing more turned on by the minute.

406

When he tried to grab Sadiya again, she batted his hand away. And he came away with a nasty scratch for his efforts.

Sadiya looked at Muhammad's midsection, and saw the alarming bulge there. Perplexed, she looked up at her husband. The disturbing smile on his handsome countenance refused to go away...

"When I was studying in the United States, I met a kind of woman that the American infidels call a dominatrix, I see the same fire in your eyes, my wife," Muhammad said, and just like that, he sat down on a chair, and his demeanor changed.

His blazing anger vanished, replaced by an air of relaxation that Sadiya had not seen in her husband in quite some time. What was going on through his head ?

407

"Husband, I am a good wife, I have obeyed you in all things and honored you, why do you provoke me so ? Do I not please you ?" Sadiya asked, her tone filled with distress, and she looked at the mark on her husband's arm and her heart ached for him.

Sadiya was perplexed by Muhammad's behavior. If she hadn't feared for her safety she never would have done this to him.

Muhammad looked at the scratch on his arm, and winced, and Sadiya went to him, eager to apologize and mend his wound, cursing herself for reacting in this manner.

"That's the thing, Sadiya, I don't want an obedient Muslim wife, I want one with fire," Muhammad said, and he rose and started toward her, and Sadiya flinched, but stood her ground.
408

Tenderly, Muhammad touched Sadiya's lovely face, and the young Saudi woman smiled, and then kissed her husband's fingers.

"I will ease your suffering," Sadiya said to Muhammad. Excusing herself, she went to get some band aids and returned a few moments later.

After tending to the scratch mark on her dear husband Muhammad's arm, Sadiya sat near him, awaiting his pleasure, so to speak.

"Husband, whatever you need of me, I will do it," Sadiya said, and her heart skipped a beat when the disturbing light came back in Muhammad's eyes.

Muhammad gestured for Sadiya to come closer, and after a brief hesitation, she did as she was told and sat beside her husband.

Muhammad looked at his wife, and sighed. They'd been married for six months and Sadiya had done everything he wanted, in and out of the bedroom.

She cooked, cleaned, helped him with his workload by doing research, and also encouraged him in all things. Could she handle his true nature ?

"Sadiya, my wife, I have a secret," Muhammad began, and Sadiya bit her lip, bracing herself for the worst.

In Saudi Arabia, a land where women are eternally at the mercy of their husbands and male family members, a woman's life is filled with tension.

A woman cannot have a close friendship with a male outside her family, otherwise she might be accused of sexual impropriety and then executed. The women always paid the price for men's folly...

"I am listening, my dear husband, whatever it is, we will face it together," Sadiya heard herself say. What could he be hiding ? Sadiya wondered. Was Muhammad out there exploring lust with males ? Did he have other women ? Was he seeing prostitutes ? Did he have a sexually transmitted disease ? Did he get fired from the Royal Engineering College of Saudi Arabia, where he was teaching part-time ? Had he grown tired of her and was he demanding a divorce ? Her

411

lips trembling, Sadiya awaited her husband's words, like a good Saudi Arabian Muslim wife should.

"Alright, Sadiya, while I was in America I explored lots of sexual activities with different kind of women, including dominant women in the world of BDSM, I discovered that I am submissive, I like being dominated by women, and, well, sometimes, I fantasize about being dominated by you," Muhammad said sheepishly, and that's when Sadiya's jaw hit the floor.

If lightning had struck the poor young Saudi Arabian Muslim right then and there, it wouldn't have shocked her more.

Sadiya looked at her hubby Muhammad like he had two heads. She was definitely not expecting that...

"So, you do not care to have an obedient Muslim wife, you want me to be bossy and controlling like those Infidel whores ?" Sadiya asked, and Muhammad nodded.

Sadiya fell silent, and looked away. Muhammad shook his head, wishing he had not told her a damn thing.

Sometimes, Muhammad wished he could have stayed in America and married Candy Jackson, the Jamaican-born student and part-time dominatrix whom he met while attending UCLA.

What a pair Muhammad and Candy would have made. A tall, bronze-skinned and dark-haired, bearded Saudi national and his short, curvy and bossy Jamaican wife...

Candy Jackson had been the one to introduce Muhammad to the world of BDSM and female domination, and his life hadn't been the same since.

Sadiya is not like Candy, Muhammad thought. Shaking his head still, Muhammad sullenly got up.

When Muhammad first met Sadiya Al-Harbi, he found her exotically beautiful with her golden brown skin and those curves and that stylish Afro which she hid under her Hijab.

He'd always found Black women gorgeous. Unfortunately, while the Black women of America were feisty and strong, Sadiya was nothing like them...

"Muhammad, did I give you permission to get up ?" Sadiya said, and something in her tone and words caused Muhammad to freeze as if someone had hit the pause button in a movie he was starring in.

When Muhammad's eyes met his wife's, Sadiya was smiling slyly and gestured imperiously with her little finger.

Muhammad smiled nervously, wondering what kind of game Sadiya was playing. He was not amused...

"Um, Sadiya, what are you doing ?" Muhammad asked, and Sadiya grinned, and walked up to him, moving in a deliberately sexy manner, a haughty look on her beautiful brown face.

Instead of answering her husband, Sadiya slapped him kind of hard in the butt, and Muhammad winced.

Looking into Sadiya's chestnut eyes, Muhammad saw a dangerous light in there, and his dick hardened swiftly. Grabbing her husband's erection, Sadiya licked her lips.

"Muhammad, it's high time I showed you who's the boss around here, this is my house, and everything inside of it is mine, including you, now, come along," Sadiya retorted, and she led Muhammad by the dick, all the way to the bedroom.

Once in there, Sadiya showed him the true essence of Black female strength, sensuality and domination. Muhammad was lucky he survived the experience...

416

"Ow, that hurts," Muhammad whined, and the tall, burly Saudi Arabian engineer found himself in a precarious position.

Muhammad is on all fours, face down and ass up, as his wife Sadiya worked her gloved fist up his asshole while stroking his cock and balls with her other hand.

Sadiya laughed and stopped stroking her hubby's jewels for a bit, and smacked his ass, causing him to groan. Little did he know that his pained screams were sweet music to her ears...

"Muhammad, shut up, we both know you love this," Sadiya shouted, and Muhammad whimpered, then fell silent.

Truth be told, he was having the time of his life. After sucking his dick and licking his balls until

417

he came, Sadiya shocked Muhammad further by draining him of his cum and licking it all up.

Afterwards, she straddled him and rode his dick so hard that he thought her pussy was made of velvet-sheathed iron. Yeah, Sadiya was a lot freakier than Muhammad could have imagined...

"Yes, Sadiya, you're the boss," Muhammad grumbled, and Sadiya gleefully continued fisting her husband's asshole.

The tough Saudi Arabian brother was like putty in her hands, and she was absolutely loving this experience.

Suddenly, Sadiya pulled her gloved fist out of Muhammad's asshole, and he gasped in surprise, turning to look at her, a puzzled look on his face.

"Now you get to eat my ass," Sadiya said, and with that, she got on all fours, and spread her thick ass cheeks wide open.

When Muhammad didn't react fast enough, Sadiya clucked her tongue. The Saudi stud got the hint, and brought his handsome mug close to his dear wife's big round butt.

Inhaling Sadiya's ass funk, Muhammad began to salivate, and slid his tongue into her butt hole. Just like that, he proceeded to eat his wife's asshole like a hungry man...

"Hmm, I do love this ass," Muhammad murmured, and he buried his tongue deep inside Sadiya's asshole.

Sadiya giggled, loving the way Muhammad's tongue felt inside her asshole. At last, the rather

After applying some Aveeno cream on Sadiya's puckered asshole, Muhammad pressed his dick against her backdoor and pushed it inside.

A sharp squeal escaped Sadiya's full lips as Muhammad's thick cock entered her warm, tight asshole.

Smacking her big light brown ass with one hand and holding her hip with the other, Muhammad began to fuck Sadiya with gusto, just the way she liked it. Nice to go back to tradition after a night of kink...

"Sadiya, shut up and give me that fat ass of yours, and twerk while you're at it," Muhammad screamed, and Sadiya turned around and flashed him a wicked grin, then did as she was told.

Sadiya began undulating her big ass, grinding it against Muhammad's groin as he continued fucking her.

Sadiya moaned and groaned, fingering her wet, hairy pussy as Muhammad's cock filled her asshole. Her husband worked her over until she came, shrieking in orgasmic delight...

"Hmm, today was definitely a day for discoveries, to many more days like this one, hubby dearest," Sadiya said to Muhammad, a few hours later, as they lay in bed.

Muhammad smiled and took Sadiya's hand, then brought it to his lips. The twenty-something Saudi Arabian engineer was smiling from ear to ear.

The day had gone better than expected, and Muhammad thanked his lucky stars to have a woman like Sadiya as his wife.

Elated after the day's events, Muhammad was still grinning when Sadiya let loose a loud, wet fart, and then went to sleep.

Welcome to the grim realities of married life, Muhammad told himself, trying not to suffocate while trying to sleep.

OBEDIENT MUSLIM HUSBANDS

"Obedient Muslim Husbands, now that's a concept that needs to be promoted more heavily," Rana Ali said to herself, in a rather smug, self-satisfied tone.

The six-foot-tall, curvy, brown-skinned, raven-haired young Kuwaiti Arab Muslim woman smiled to herself.

Sitting on a throne-like chair in the living room of her plush townhouse in the City of Al Farwaniyah, State of Kuwait, Rana Ali was immensely pleased with herself.

The beautiful Queen of the manor awaited the arrival of her King, and yearned to do nasty things to him...

After six and a half months of being married to a handsome Kuwaiti Muslim heir named Khalid Sabah, Rana Ali had settled into the lifestyle of a wealthy Kuwaiti Arab Muslim housewife.

Her days were spent on lavish shopping, and wandering the City of Al Farwaniyah, with the occasional trip to Paris, France, or London, UK, to break up the monotony every few months.

Rana's hunky husband Khalid kept her financially stable and sexually satisfied, like a good husband should...

Returning to her native Kuwait after four years spent studying at Carleton University in the City of Ottawa, Ontario, Rana Ali experienced a bold new world.

The Western world had its vices and troubles, but in Canada, no one cared that Rana Ali was born of a Kuwaiti Arab Muslim father and of a Saudi Arabian mother.

In Kuwaiti society, while intercultural and interracial marriages did occur, most families preferred to have their sons and daughters marry not only their own country folk, but also members of their own tribe.

That's why so many people in Kuwait City were stunned when Rana's father, Sheikh Amir Ali, married a young Saudi Arabian woman, Afaf Qasim of Dammam.

Rana Ali grew up hearing from many sources how she wasn't a true Kuwaiti since her mother was a foreign woman.

To the Canadians, Rana Ali was just another young Arab woman out and about, doing her thing, and they paid her little heed.

While in the City of Ottawa, Rana studied civil engineering and upon returning to the City of Al Farwaniyah, she had grand ambitions.

Rana wasn't satisfied with the idea of playing wife to some wealthy Kuwaiti Muslim man whose every thought was mired in Arabian cultural norms and Islamic rules.

Nope, Rana had to have things her way, like a true woman of the world. In her Universe, women rule and men obey.

That's why Rana ran her own business, a small bookstore with a cyber café, and hired two young Ethiopian women to help her run it.

When Rana wasn't at work, or gossiping with her employees, or shopping, she ran the Sabah household with an iron fist.

"Yes my lady," replied a deep, measured male voice, and Rana looked at her husband Khalid Sabah, a tall and burly man with caramel-hued skin, slick curly Black hair and a thick beard.

Striding into the living room, clad in a stylish Thobe, Khalid was a vision of masculine beauty.

Rana Ali felt a tingle in her womanly core as Khalid stepped forward, and bowed gently.

"Welcome home, dear husband," Rana Ali said, and she grabbed Khalid Sabah and kissed him, after giving his butt a firm squeeze of course.

Rana had a lot of truly nasty things she wanted to do to her favorite guy. Khalid grinned as Rana all but pounced on him, hornier than ever after the few hours they spent apart. *What a woman*, Khalid thought, amazed.

Khalid Sabah was born in the City of Salwa, Kuwait, to a Kuwaiti Arab Muslim father and an African mother originally from the City of Dakar, Senegal.

When Khalid's parents, Omar Sabah and Yasmin Camara got married, many members of the upper echelons of Kuwaiti society found their interracial and intercultural union quite scandalous.

Khalid's parents didn't care, and they raised their only son to be strong and proud, ready to defy traditionalists and haters and do his own thing.

Tall and ruggedly handsome, the product of Arabian and African bloodlines, Khalid was a formidable man. One whom Rana Ali endeavored to mold to her liking...

While Rana Ali's father, Sheikh Amir Ali, one of the leading Clerics of the Kuwaiti National Judiciary sent her to study at a Canadian University, fate sent Khalid on the opposite direction.

Khalid's father, Imam Omar Sabah sent him to study at the prestigious King Abdullah University of Science and Technology in the City of Thuwal, deep inside the Kingdom of Saudi Arabia.

The young biracial Kuwaiti found the Western-style school quite odd with its coed classes and Western-style way of doing things.

After obtaining his business management degree, Khalid Sabah returned to Kuwait, fed up with the Western women he met while at K.A.U.

Of course, the young biracial Kuwaiti wasn't totally honest with himself about his time spent in Saudi Arabia.

While there, Khalid met a lively young woman named Soraya Ahmed. Born in the United States of America to a Somali Muslim father and a White American mother, Soraya was uniquely beautiful, smart and ambitious.

After studying economics at the University of Minnesota, Soraya Ahmed decided to explore life outside the Western world, and opted to study for a year at the prestigious King Abdullah University of Science and Technology in Saudi Arabia.

While studying at K.A.U. Soraya met an interesting young man named Khalid Sabah. In spite of their differences, Soraya and Khalid ended up becoming friends, and later, falling in love.

Soraya was the one who introduced Khalid to the world of BDSM and female domination. The woman who changed his world.

Khalid Sabah, a wealthy young man who grew up pampered and privileged in Kuwait, a land where men had absolute authority over their women, thanks to Islamic cultural norms, became fascinated with female domination.

Soraya introduced Khalid to the world of female domination and male submission, and he learned to enjoy getting spanked, flogged, and even fucked in the ass with a strap-on dildo.

Khalid thought he put such pursuits behind him after graduating from K.A.U. and returning to his native Kuwait. Fate indeed had other plans for the young biracial Kuwaiti...

While Khalid continued to miss his former classmate and Mistress, the lovely and unforgettable Soraya Ahmed, fate intervened by providing him with a lovely replacement.

From the get go, Khalid knew that his new bride Rana Ali was beautiful, entitled, demanding and at times, downright bossy.

He would soon found out how bossy she could be when one of his most carefully guarded secrets finally unraveled.

The lady of a house always finds out everything that goes on in said house, after all. Such is the way of the world.

"I found a lot of porn magazines in your bags, and they feature women tying men up and beating them, what's up with that, Habibi?" Rana Ali asked her husband Khalid Sabah when he came home from work one day, a few months after their wedding day.

Khalid looked at his incensed wife Rana, who clutched the Femdom magazines in her hand, an angry look upon her beautiful face.

"Oh, that's nothing, Habibiti, I swear upon Jannah, these magazines belonged to my old roommate Hamid, and somehow got into my luggage," Khalid replied sheepishly, and Rana Ali looked at the tall, dark and handsome biracial Kuwaiti Muslim heir, shaking her lovely head.

Men all act the same way when busted doing something illicit, Rana thought, wryly amused by her husband Khalid's behavior. This was going to be so much fun...

"Khalid Sabah, don't lie to me, you like to walk around like you're a king, but deep down, you like being dominated by women, like those Infidel men on those websites on the Internet, stop lying and admit it," Rana Ali said, arms crossed and eyes blazing with anger.

The young Kuwaiti Arab Muslim woman walked up to her husband and jabbed him really hard in the chest.

When he blinked in surprise, Rana whacked him upside the head. Khalid rubbed his head, and flinched. What the fuck ?

"Alright, I admit, I find those websites arousing, and those Femdom magazines are mine," Khalid admitted, and much to his surprise, Rana Ali's expression softened.

The young woman gently wrapped her arms around her husband, and rested her head against his shoulder.

The two of them held each other like this for a long moment before Rana Ali finally broke the silence.

"Khalid Sabah, you are my husband and I love you, if you're having sexual fantasies of being dominated by a woman, I want to be that woman, I will

435

dominate you, if that's what makes you happy,"
Rana Ali said, looking into her husband's eyes.

Khalid Sabah looked at his wife and smiled,
nodding quite eagerly. The young biracial Kuwaiti
Muslim heir could not believe his luck.

Rana smiled triumphantly, determined to own her
husband's mind, body and soul...and she would let
nothing get in her way.

"Yes, flog me, Rana," Khalid squealed as he found
himself bent over the sofa, and Rana flogged his
buttocks and back with his own belt.

Laughing, Rana eagerly whooped her husband's ass,
loving the way it jiggled every time she struck it
with the belt.

When Rana told her friends and family of her
intent to marry Khalid, many of them objected, for

he was born of an Arab father and an African mother, and thusly wasn't a pure Kuwaiti.

Rana found Khalid handsome, smart and sexy, and refused to change her mind. In the end, Rana's family and friends accepted her choice of mate. And now, Khalid was hers...

"I own you, you crazy beautiful man," Rana whispered into Khalid's ear, as she stopped flogging and began fondling his big dark dick with one hand while caressing his cute ass with the other.

Khalid gasped as Rana began fingering his asshole, and upon noticing that having his ass played with turned Khalid on, Rana added a second finger into his bum.

After a while, Rana inserted a thick candle into Khalid's ass and twisted it around, causing him to moan and groan.

"Fuck me," Khalid moaned, as Rana smacked his ass and shoved the candle deeper and deeper into his asshole.

Turning Khalid around, Rana made him lie on his back and stroked his dick while fucking his ass with the candle.

When Khalid warned that he was about to cum, Rana took his dick into her mouth and sucked him dry. Khalid came, and Rana welcomed the torrent of liquid masculinity that rushed down her throat.

"Eat my ass and maybe I'll let you fuck me," Rana Ali told Khalid, and the young man nodded and smiled.

Rana got on all fours and shook her big Arabian booty at her hubby. Khalid came up behind her and smiled, then caressed her butt.

Spreading Rana's thick ass cheeks wide open, Khalid began to eat his wife's asshole, loving the way it smelled and tasted.

Rana moaned softly, fingering her wet pussy as Khalid ate her ass. The brother voraciously licked her asshole and didn't let up until she cried out his name...

"Whose booty is this ?" Khalid screamed, a little while later, as he put Rana on all fours and showed his feisty wife who's boss.

Rana squealed in delight as Khalid slammed his thick dark dick into her. Now that's what she really craved...

Every woman wants her man to be strong, in and out of the bedroom. This holds true Universally, regardless of the races, cultures and locations involved...

The biracial stud fucked her with an ardor worthy of both his sturdy African and fierce Arabian ancestry, and Rana kept grinding her big brown booty against his groin, and she absolutely loved it.

"That ass is yours, my king," Rana squealed, and Khalid grabbed her long dark hair, which was sans Hijab for a change, and fucked her silly.

Slapping Rana's thick ass while fucking, Khalid dutifully rammed his hard dick into her wet, hot pussy.

Khalid fucked his wife with passion and didn't let up until they both lost count of how many times they came, and lay, exhausted, on soaked bedsheets.

Rana looked at Khalid and grinned, pleased to see that her king had at last come home, in every way...

"I am lucky to have you, my dear Rana," Khalid said, and a smiling Rana rested her head against her hubby's chest.

Outside, in the streets of Al Farwaniyah, a desert storm raged, and most people were understandably hurrying home. Rana Ali and Khalid Sabah couldn't care less, for a veritable storm of passion was brewing in their bedroom.

Having swiftly recovered from their previous lovemaking, Rana and Khalid swiftly began another round.

Passion makes the world go around and a strong Muslim woman is a wonderful treasure for a worthwhile Muslim man who accepts her.

Just ask Khalid Sabah of Kuwait, a young Muslim man who has the immense pleasure, and sometime

441

burden of being married to such a sultry, bossy lady...

LOVE IN THE CITY OF LIGHTS

The sun rose over the City of Paris, France, bathing the City of Lights in its penetrating golden haze.

Salwa "Sal" Taher stretched luxuriously on the king-sized bed in the master bedroom of her rented townhouse in the rather plush Neuilly-Sur-Seine neighborhood.

The young woman yawned, and then got up, and stood in front of the mirror, wearing only a coy smile on her lovely face.

Pure satisfaction was etched on her features, and with good reason. She was still glowing from a really, really good fuck...

After a night of passion during which Sal got very little rest, there were dark circles under her eyes.

Sal felt pleasurably sore all over, her curvy body still tingly from all the fun and wicked things she'd done with her lover.

Thankfully, she only had one afternoon class at the Sorbonne campus of the University of Paris. Morning classes quite simply weren't her style.

Sal liked to wake up for Fajr prayer, and then she went right back to snoozing. Nothing else was waking up early for...

Sal glanced outside the nearby window, and admired la belle cite. The City of Paris was covered in a fine sheen of snow, and Sal, who hailed from the Kingdom of Saudi Arabia, land of the burning sands, shivered inwardly.

As much as she loved living in Europe, she'd never get used to the snow. The cold seemed unnatural to her, a woman who was native to a land that had never known frost in the past ten thousand years...

Sal closed her eyes briefly, remembering life in her homeland, which had its own beauty in spite of the social restrictions that both men and women faced, due to the strictest interpretations of Islam's rules.

Salwa missed the Kingdom of Saudi Arabia, its simplicity and beauty, the sturdy but decent, honest people.

In Paris, France, things were different. Sal had far more freedom in this place, sure, but like women the world over, she had to seek opportunity while being ever weary of pitfalls...

In Saudi Arabia, everyone knew what everyone was. The royal family ruled the nation and controlled the oil refineries and thusly ran the economy, and underneath them were the endless groups of religious clerics and government officials.

The bureaucratic class. In the Kingdom of Saudi Arabia, religion and government were virtually one, intricately bound and interwoven.

Everyone who wasn't a royal or some kind of cleric/bureaucratic government worker was at the bottom...

There were other aspects of life inside the Kingdom that Salwa never questioned, until she went to live in another country.

The way that Saudis treated African minorities living among them was atrocious, and they didn't treat the Filipino and South Asian workers who worked in the construction sector any better.

In Saudi Arabia, there had never been a women's rights movement or a civil rights movement, so women and racial minorities continued to be little more than chattel, forever at the mercy of Saudi Arabian men.

After all, Saudi Arabia is the last country in the world to officially outlaw the practice of slavery, in the year 1962.

In the Saudi realm, men made the decisions and women obeyed, or so it would seem to the casual observer. Behind closed doors, and in the corridors of power, however, Saudi women wielded a great deal of influence.

446

They were outpacing their men in international education, for example. The future of Saudi Arabia was female, pure and simple.

Salwa herself was in Paris because a group of her Saudi foremothers persuaded the Saudi government to invest in education, and thus their nation's future.

They accomplished this by sending Saudi students, male and female, to study abroad in American, Canadian, Australian and European schools, to help develop the Saudi economy.

Sal remembered her early days in Paris, which seemed like a different world compared to Saudi Arabia.

The people, the weather, the way Frenchmen and women mingled freely, and the absence of the Mutaween or religious police, enforcer of rigid gender-based apartheid, all this seemed strange yet wonderful to her.

To the initially naïve, dreamy-eyed Salwa, Paris seemed like a dream come true, and then she learned better...

Like all modern cities, Paris is home to all kinds of souls, the good and the bad, the beautiful and the ugly.

Sal met many fellow Muslims there, people from places like Somalia, Algeria, Morocco, Kuwait, Kenya, Nigeria, Indonesia, Pakistan, and so on.

She attended school at U of P and also went to meetings of the local Muslim Scholars Association. *Always searching for a place to belong*, Salwa thought bitterly.

At school, Sal made friends, and enemies. Some of the French students were openly hostile to her, simply for being a Hijab-wearing Muslim woman from the Middle East.

Others were so friendly, they seemed almost heavenly. The City of Paris was a mix of the angelic and the devilish, and Sal hastily learned to discern between the two.

Loneliness continued to plague Salwa, until a certain handsome, persistent young man came into her life, three years ago...

"Sal, reviens au lit, come back to bed," a sleepy male voice called out, and Salwa smiled but did not turn.

Instead, Salwa watched as a certain big and tall, dark-skinned young man sat up on the bed, stark naked, and wiped the sleep from his eyes.

Marcel Duchene yawned, and then fixed his gaze on Sal...and that's when he took a deep breath, pausing.

The voluptuous, bronze-skinned and raven-haired young woman, originally from the City of Dhahran, Saudi Arabia, was definitely a sight for sore eyes...

"Nah, come to me," Sal murmured, and she then proceeded to ensure that Marcel, a handsome and charming but stubborn Haitian stud, complied with her demand.

She 'accidentally' knocked a hairbrush from the lower shelf of the dresser in front of her, and then bent down to pick it up.

The effect was immediate, for if Marcel had one weakness, it was a thick round ass, and Sal's was definitely one of the best that he'd ever seen...

"Come here, ma belle," Marcel said, laughing as he pulled Salwa into his arms. She wouldn't get away so easily...

Giggling, the young woman tried to get away, but strong arms wrapped themselves gently but firmly around her, preventing her escape.

Marcel kissed the back of her neck and sniffed her raven hair, which smelled great even before she did her morning routine.

Marcel's hands went from Sal's waist to her buttocks, and she licked her lips as he gave her thick ass cheeks a firm squeeze.

"Hmm, Habibi, is every man from the island of Haiti addicted to big girly bums or just you ?" Sal asked, and she turned around, facing Marcel.

The brother smiled, and playfully slapped her ass, then took her face into his hands. Sal looked up at

Marcel, who, at six-foot-four, was exactly one foot taller than her.

Like so many women from the Heartland of Islam, Salwa Taher was short, curvy, dark-eyed, dark-haired and bronze-skinned, seemingly soft and sweet but hardy, as befitting a daughter of the desert.

"Hmm, I'm one of a kind," Marcel replied, and Sal grinned, and stood on her tippy toes, planting a wet kiss on his full, succulent lips.

Sal tasted Marcel's morning breath, and did not care. Passionately they embraced, and then began making love.

Marcel lifted Sal up, causing her to squeal. He smiled and proceeded to caress her breasts, teasing her by flicking his tongue over her erect nipples.

Sal held her breath as Marcel spread her thick thighs, and then knelt before her, as if to worship at her altar...

"Um, uh," Sal managed to croak out, before Marcel buried his face between her legs and began eating her pussy.

Salwa felt a bit self-conscious because she hadn't showered yet, but Marcel most definitely did not care.

The brother ate her pussy like a hungry man, teasing her clit with his tongue and sliding his fingers into her, twisting them this way and that, causing Sal to squeal in delight.

The young woman went wild, her body shuddering with pleasure as her lover worked his magic on her...

"Just relax and enjoy, Habibti," Marcel paused to say, and Sal nodded hastily, closing her eyes as her lover did his thing.

Later, he bent her over the nearby sofa, and as she expected, he proceeded to worship her ass. On all fours, Sal moaned softly as Marcel slid a finger into her butt hole even as he continued to give her pussy a serious tongue lashing.

"Hmm, I want to taste you," Sal said, for she was eager to return the favor after Marcel made her pussy squirt, time and again, and made her scream so loud, she was sure her neighbors heard her.

Marcel nodded as Sal grabbed his dick, which was long, thick and dark. Like many men from the Caribbean and Latin America, Marcel was uncircumcised, something which Sal, as a Muslim woman, initially found strange, but quickly got over.

454

Indeed, she found his 'hooded' dick quite fun to play with...

"Dammit, Salwa, you're killing a brother," Marcel cried out as Sal tugged on his ball sac while fellating him, greedily.

Marcel watched as the young Saudi Arabian Muslim woman, who seemed so prim and proper when he met her during his first year at the University of Paris suck his dick like there was no tomorrow.

When Marcel had enough, he had to basically pull Sal off of his manhood, because she simply refused to let go.

"You belong to me, handsome," Salwa said as she practically pounced on Marcel, and the Haitian hunk tumbled on the carpeted floor, surprised by the curvy, diminutive Saudi beauty's rather fierce strength.

Sal climbed on top of Marcel, and impaled herself on his dick, sighing deeply as he was finally embedded within her.

Marcel smiled and bucked his hips, thrusting into her, and Sal began to scream, loving the feel of his hard, throbbing manhood inside of her...

"I can't get enough of you, and your killer derriere, ma Cherie," Marcel said, as he put Sal on all fours, and fucked her like this.

Sal screamed passionately as Marcel fucked her with wild abandon, slamming his hard dick into her.

She gave as good as she got, grinding her ample derriere against her lover's groin, driving his dick deeper inside of her.

The two lovers continued to fuck and suck well into the latter part of the morning, only stopping when exhaustion finally claimed them...

Salwa Taher, born in Saudi Arabia to a family of Judicial Clerics, sighed happily as she sat at the table with her lover Marcel Duchene.

The Haitian stud had truly outdone himself this time. After they finished making love, she went to shower, and meanwhile, he went and got breakfast for them at a small nearby café.

Salwa and Marcel feasted on a breakfast composed of omelets, buttered bread, oat cakes, and overly sugared coffee...plus what passes for pita bread in France.

"Merci pour ce dcjeuner de roi, thank you for this royal breakfast," Sal said, in passable French, and

Marcel took her hand and gently kissed it, then winked at her while sipping his coffee.

Looking at the handsome young man sitting opposite her, Sal smiled, feeling pure contentment. No one in Sal's life had ever made her feel as loved or appreciated as Marcel did, that's for damn sure.

To many more days like this one, Salwa thought. Instead of worrying about the future, about the world she left behind and would eventually have to return to, she decided to enjoy the only thing she knew for sure, the day she was currently in.

Smiling at Marcel, Sal gently placed her hand on top of his, and nodded firmly before she resumed eating.

Today, they'd go hang out, perhaps dine at a fine restaurant or visit the Louvre, and then, upon returning home, more lovemaking. Life was good...for now.

WAFA ALI OF SAUDI ARABIA

"Joseph, I have to warn you, if you keep hanging around me, I might convert you to Islam," Wafa "Wawa" Ali said, and the curvy, bronze-skinned and raven-haired young Saudi Arabian Muslim woman smiled coyly at her friend and classmate, Joseph Berry.

The tall, slender, Afro-sporting, brown-skinned young man, originally from the City of London, U.K. looked at her and shook his head. *Fat chance of that happening,* Joseph thought with a smirk.

459

As much as Joseph liked Wawa, who was turning out to be quite different from what he expected, especially given her nationality and religion, Joseph had no desire to enter her rather complicated and mystifying world.

Besides, he met Wawa at a very peculiar time in his life. His relationship with a certain big-bottomed Jamaican beauty named Carole Hawthorne had ended, abruptly.

Right now, Joseph was bored, restless, semi-depressed, and, as befitting a young man of his years, ever horny...

"Nope, Wawa, you're tripping, my friend," Joseph replied, and upon hearing his response, Wawa simply smiled at him, and winked confidently.

The two of them sat inside the Brighton University library, one dour Sunday evening in late November.

For a London lad like Joseph, southern England was boring as can be, and not for the first time he regretted the fact that his parents, Luther Berry and Julianne Brinkley-Berry sent him there.

Joseph was having too wild a time at Cambridge, and they banished him to this third-rate school, where he was surrounded by rural types...

"Joseph, habibi, Saudi Arabian women like myself are addictive," Wawa said, and with that, she licked her full lips, a gesture which registered with a certain part of Joseph's anatomy.

The young biracial man shifted in his seat, and crossed his legs, and Wawa, noticing his discomfort, flashed him a smile a shark would recognize.

They were supposed to be working on their assignment, *Death Penalty In England*, for their political science class, but they were too busy flirting instead...

"Wawa, if I keep listening to you, I might actually fail this class," Joseph replied, and Wawa laughed and playfully slapped his arm. Joseph chuckled softly.

It was astonishing how familiar they'd become with one another. Boundaries such as religion and cultural quickly fell out the window once he and Wawa got to know each other.

All that remained, once the smoke cleared, was the two of them, a taciturn man and an incredibly feisty woman...

Joseph met Wawa a couple of months ago, while working as a tour guide for the Brighton University Office of International Students.

That's where he met the twenty-something, seemingly reserved, Hijab-wearing and outwardly pious newcomer from the Kingdom of Saudi Arabia.

The one with the lovely brown eyes and coy smile. Joseph, a prim and proper English lad, felt a stir in certain parts of himself when Wawa looked at him. Puzzled, he felt drawn to this mysterious woman...

As fate and luck would have it, Joseph and Wawa ended up in the same political science class, and aside from the contract instructor, Mr. Raj Singh, they were the only non-Whites there.

In this small town of Brighton, barely two hours away from the City of London proper, Joseph and Wawa felt like a couple of aliens.

The people of Brighton weren't used to dealing with Africans, Arabs, Asians and others. And they didn't mind showing it to such people, in various ways, when they encountered them...

For these and many other reasons, Joseph and Wawa began hanging out together, as ethnic oddities in a largely homogenous English town.

They bonded over shared stories of uncomfortable moments spent dealing with these rural English folk, who weren't shy about telling them to go back to the city.

The two strangers became close friends, united by adversity, like soldiers hunkering in the same bunker, with bombs falling all around them...

"Joseph, habibi, the Creator made mankind strong, but He also made womankind both strong and wise, you should do as I say," Wawa said and Joseph nodded, and then looked out the window pensively.

Wawa fell silent, having a pretty clear guess as to where Joseph's thoughts went. He's thinking about his ex-girlfriend again, Wawa thought, and for some reason, her heart winced.

"I've made some foolish decisions recently that's for sure, especially when it comes to women," Joseph said, and when he looked at Wawa, and saw the concern on her lovely face, he flashed her a meek smile and shrugged.

He acted as though nothing bothered him, but his lady friend knew better. Wawa drew closer to Joseph, and all the concern and affection that she felt for this annoyingly charming, or charmingly annoying, taciturn young infidel bubbled to the surface.

"Joseph, I know your pain, Wallahi, believe me, I left behind a country, and a husband who mistreated me, and had to start from scratch, believe me, you can get over a lot of things," Wawa said, and Joseph looked at her, and he could have sworn her lovely brown eyes looked moist.

Wawa smiled, sniffed, and then gently laid her hand on his shoulder, then got up and gave him a meaningful look before walking away.

Joseph sat there and watched Wawa walk away, and for a brief moment, he was struck by something which should have occurred to him a long time ago.

Wawa is amazing, and she cares about me, Joseph thought with a start. It struck him like lightning, that realization...

In that moment, Joseph stopped thinking about his ex, and his eyes, mind and soul focused on a certain short, curvy, big-bottomed, Hijab-wearing cutie who was soon vanishing from his line of sight...

"I always end up with the wrong man," Wawa said to herself as she hurried back to her on-campus residence, and she bit back a sob.

Wawa thought of her old life in Dammam, in the Eastern Province of Saudi Arabia. Ten years ago, nineteen-year-old Wawa married Hafiz Alharbi, the son of a wealthy Saudi family from Medina.

At first, Hafiz seemed charming, but later, he turned out to be abusive and controlling. In the end, their relationship proved unbearable for Wawa, and they got divorced.

That was a long time ago, and Wawa was a different person back then. Following her divorce, Wawa left Saudi Arabia and lived in Canada for a time, studying business at Concordia University in the City of Montreal, Quebec.

After graduating with her business degree, Wawa returned to Saudi Arabia and worked as a money keeper for Bin Hassan, one of the biggest financial institutions in her country.

Feeling unsatisfied about her career prospects, Wawa left the Kingdom of Saudi Arabia, this time for the United Kingdom.

After applying to London's Cambridge University and getting rejected, Wawa opted for her second choice, Brighton University, where she met a most remarkable young man...one with smoldering eyes who made her heart go pitter-patter.

Wawa surprised herself when she started to develop feelings for Joseph, who was pretty charming when he wanted to be...

Wawa smiled to herself as she recalled those times when she walked around the Stratford City Mall in London with Joseph.

Arm in arm, they walked through various stores, in the world-class city featured in so many movies and novels.

Joseph, a native Londoner, showed his hometown to Wawa, taking her to malls, movie theaters, restaurants, museums and the like, and in time, she fell in love with London...and with him.

Sadly, the lad couldn't shut up about what's-her-face. Sheesh ! Wawa threw enough hints Joseph's way to write a book !

Joseph sat there, and watched Wawa walk away, and that's when it hit him like a ton of bricks. *Wawa really does care about me, underneath all the sarcasm, and I've been blathering on about my ex*

469

like an idiot, Joseph thought, and he grinned and shook his head.

By the time he got to his feet, however, a certain curvy, short and gorgeous Saudi gal was well on her way out of the Brighton University library...

Wawa went to her on-campus flat, and once there, she took a shower. Her one-bedroom apartment was nothing fancy, especially since she was paying half the rent, the other half was paid for by the Saudi Ministry of Education.

Wawa signed a deal with them that she would come back to Saudi Arabia with her new British University degree, and put it to work for the economic and social well-being of her country. Well, that was the plan anyway...

If Wawa were honest with herself, she would have to admit that she'd grown fond of life outside Saudi Arabia.

She loved her homeland, but felt very little attachment to it these days. Her parents were dead, and her ex-husband and his family cursed her very existence.

Wawa always dreamed of starting a new life in the West somewhere, but these days, people in places like Canada, America, Australia and the United Kingdom seemed to hate Muslims...

The Kingdom of Saudi Arabia seemed like a prison for women, at least that's how many western feminists described it.

Wawa loved her homeland, and she remembered her parents, Wahid and Noor Ali quite fondly. They were wonderful and loving people.

471

Wawa also remembered her neighbors, and her first love, a tall, dark and handsome young Sudanese Muslim worker named Mahfouz.

This had been her first exposure to men of African descent, and it was an experience which changed Wawa's life...

When Wawa Ali met Joseph Berry at Brighton University, she'd been astonished at how much the twenty-one-year-old Londoner, born of a Jamaican immigrant father and a White British mother, resembled her lost love, Mahfouz.

They were indeed very different men, of course. Mahfouz was a free spirit while Joseph was no-nonsense, too moody and serious for his own good.

Wawa remembered the passionate nights she spent with Mahfouz, during that last summer before she was made to marry that idiot Alharbi.

472

Sitting on the couch, watching *The Great British Bake-Off* on Channel 4, Wafa thought of her lost love Mahfouz.

Wawa smiled to herself as she recalled how she felt in Mahfouz's arms. Loved, safe, and absolutely wanted.

The tall, bearded, dark-skinned and strongly built Afro-Arabian brother kissed her passionately, as if he would never kiss her again, as they embraced in a backroom inside her parents villa...

"Ente Jamile Masha'Allah, you are so beautiful," Mahfouz said as he tenderly stroked Wafa's lovely face.

Wafa threw her arms around Mahfouz's torso, and sighed happily as he drew her to a nearby table, hoisted her on it, and proceeded to make love to her.

It was not the most comfortable, but she didn't care one bit.

When she felt Mahfouz's hands on her breasts, Wafa smiled and took off her abaya, revealing her nakedness to him.

"I am yours, Habibi, my love," Wafa replied, and Mahfouz kissed her lips while caressing her breasts, his agile tongue sliding down her throat.

Wafa sighed happily as Mahfouz worked his magic on her, his mouth moving to her throat, and then to her breasts.

She felt a pleasant tingle when his tongue flicked over her areolas, and then Mahfouz slid his hand between her thighs.

Wafa held her breath as her lover's sleek but strong fingers wormed their way into her womanhood...

474

"Habibti, relax and enjoy," Mahfouz murmured into Wafa's ear, and the young woman smiled nervously and nodded.

This was her first time being made love to, her first time knowing a man's touch. A defining moment in any woman's life...

In the Kingdom of Saudi Arabia, where the Arabs still hold unfavorable views of the Blacks, Wafa would never be permitted to marry a man of African descent, not even a fellow Muslim.

Wawa found Mahfouz of Sudan handsome, smart, passionate, caring and attentive, everything a woman wants in a man.

The holy texts of their Muslim faith had nothing against interracial relationships among Muslims, but in Arab culture, the men were allowed to marry whoever they wanted but not the women.

475

Wawa knew those draconian, unfair rules, yet her heart yearned for Mahfouz, and she craved his touch...

"Go for it, my love," Wafa whispered, and Mahfouz smiled, then spread her thighs and began pleasuring her down below with his tongue.

Wafa moaned softly, previously unimagined pleasures flooding her body and soul as Mahfouz licked her pussy, teased her clitoris with his tongue and twisted his fingers inside her core.

Wafa was like putty in his hands, and Mahfouz, a true connoisseur of lovemaking, showed her thing or two...

That night was one of passion and discovery for Wafa and Mahfouz. A wicked smile creased Wafa's face as she recalled the exact moment when her lover stood before her, stark naked, dark skin glistening in the low light, and she tentatively ran her hands over his masculine body.

Absolutely amazed by what she beheld, Wafa smiled nervously, and then took Mahfouz's manhood in her hands.

"Are you ready, my love?" Mahfouz asked, and Wafa smiled and nodded. Boldly, Mahfouz lifted her up and placed her on his lap, and then rubbed his hard member against her mound.

Wafa grasped Mahfouz's dick, and then rubbed it against her vaginal opening. With a swift thrust, he entered her, and Wafa let out a happy sigh.

At last, Wafa got to know what it was like to be a woman, and as Mahfouz's hard member filled her vagina, she cried out, singing a song of passion and thanks as he fucked her, passionately.

Without even realizing it, Wafa had begun to masturbate, right there on the couch, in her tiny on-campus apartment in southern England.

Wawa pinched her nipples and fingered her pussy, after her hand down her pants, touching a much-neglected part of herself.

The young Saudi woman was so wrapped up in self-pleasuring that she was utterly shocked when her doorbell rang, and a familiar male voice hollered.

Too distracted to actually reply, Wafa suddenly realized that she'd left her front door slightly open...

"Wafa, are you home ? The door's open, I was worried," Joseph asked as he strode in, his handsome face filled with worry.

Wafa gasped, and in her shock, she fell off the couch, and landed squarely onto her plump rump. Concerned, Joseph rushed to her aid, and caught her flagrante delicto, as they say.

The young Londoner's facial expression changed from one of worry to one of surprise mixed with embarrassment...

"Joseph, oh shit," Wafa blurted out, as she hurriedly tried to do two things at once, pull her pants back on, and get up, of course.

Joseph, the proper British gentleman, averted his eyes while offering her hand. Sighing, Wafa took Joseph's hand after a brief hesitation.

Pulling herself to her feet with his help, Wafa stood in front of Joseph, who was still looking away. In spite of the horribly embarrassing situation, Wafa smiled and tugged on Joseph's sleeve...

"Oh good, you're decent, sorry to barge in like that, I thought something had happened to you," Joseph said, and he stood in front of Wafa, looking more nervous than a cat in a room full of rocking chairs.

Wafa looked at Joseph, this tall, dark and handsome, charming young man who so resembled her lost love.

An almost identical copy of the very man Wawa had been fantasizing about all those years, and the man whose handsome face haunted her thoughts as she masturbated, just moments ago...

"Joseph, relax, we're friends, and besides, I know I'm not the first woman you've seen naked," Wawa joked, trying to make light of a horribly embarrassing situation.

Joseph fell silent, and much to Wawa's amazement, the biracial Londoner suddenly looked pale. Gently she touched his arm, and then looked into his eyes.

Joseph bit his lip, and then, sighed, something he did when he had something pressing on his rather taciturn brain...

"Wawa, Carole and I have never had sex, we were going to, but she left me for this guy named Todd," Joseph said, and he shrugged, as if he'd just admitted to chewing gum or something inane like that.

Wawa looked at him quite pensively. *A tall, handsome brother like that, and he's never been with a woman*, Wawa thought. All of a sudden, a lot of things about Joseph's behavior made sense...

"Well, Joseph, my dear, she was a fool to leave you," Wawa heard herself say, and then she drew herself on her tippy toes and kissed Joseph.

The young man seemed surprised by her kiss, but he returned it with a passion which absolutely surprised her.

When they came up for air, Wawa and Joseph looked into each other's eyes, and exchanged a smile. Hand in hand, the two best friends left the living room area, and headed for the bedroom...

"You're so beautiful," Joseph said as Wawa drew him to her bed, and then they undressed. The young man looked at his female friend's curvy body, taking in her voluptuousness, her large breasts, her sheer loveliness.

The bronze-skinned, gorgeous Arab gal looked at him, and he saw a raw passion akin to hunger in her lovely dark eyes.

Once again they kissed, and this time, Joseph took the lead, answering the call of masculine passions long subdued by his gentlemanly nature...

"Be patient, my dear, we don't need to rush," Wawa whispered into Joseph's ear as she rolled on top of him.

The young man gently caressed her face, her breasts, her round little belly, and finally her ample bum.

Wawa grinned when Joseph playfully smacked her bum, then grasped her ass cheeks. *All the sons of Africa love women with big butts,* Wawa thought with a smile.

"Oh wow, Wawa, I want you so much," Joseph said as he kissed her passionately, while his hands roamed all over her body.

Wawa straddled him, and played with his chest hairs before reaching for his manhood. Joseph was well-endowed, with a thick, hard member that was uncircumcised, so unlike those of her former lover Mahfouz and her former husband Wahid.

Nevertheless, Wawa stroked Joseph's dick, and then winked at him as a wicked idea sprang into her mind.

"I've got a little treat for you, handsome," Wawa murmured, and Joseph watched, astonished, as his lady friend kissed his lips, then his chest while stroking his dick.

Wawa kissed a path down to Joseph's groin, and then she took his dick into her mouth. Joseph held his breath as Wawa began sucking his dick.

He'd yearned for this for ages, to be pleasured in such a way by a woman, but he'd never had the chance. Now, at last, things were happening for him...

"Oh damn, Wawa, you're amazing," Joseph cried out, as Wawa's soft, warm lips engulfed his manhood, and he experienced sensations he'd previously only imagined.

As the night progressed, Wawa gave Joseph his first carnal lesson, and an introduction to the art of pleasing a woman.

Joseph put his sweet lips to good use as her Wawa's instructions, and he first sucked on her tits, then licked her sweet pussy.

The smell and taste of Wawa's womanhood was wonderfully intoxicating, and Joseph, a first-timer through and true, found it amazing...

"Now comes the moment of truth, Joseph, I want you inside of me," Wawa said, locking eyes with Joseph.

The curvy Saudi beauty lay on her back, her curvy body slick with sweat, hair a wild mess, eyes blazing with lust.

Joseph looked at her and nodded, even as he stroked his hard member. He'd never seen anyone, or anything, as beautiful as Wawa looked to him right now, that's for damn sure...

"Yes, I want this too," Joseph said, and with that, he positioned himself between Wawa's thick legs, and pushed his dick into her pussy.

He felt a brief resistance, and then he was inside her. Wawa bit her lip as Joseph's thick rod went into her, a bit too quickly, but that was to be expected.

Looking into her eyes, Joseph raised Wawa's legs in the air and continued to fuck her, and she smiled, nodding in approval.

There's hope for this one yet, Wawa thought as Joseph's noble tool filled her quite nicely, and she began to enjoy the ride, as it were...

"Fuck me harder," Wawa squealed, a little while later, as Joseph took her on all fours. Doggy style had long been her favorite sexual position, even though, in her twenty nine years, she'd only been with three men.

Third time is the charm, Wawa thought as Joseph gripped her wide hips and slammed his dick so hard into her pussy that she felt as though the London stud were trying to brand her.

They went at it like this for a bit, until, exhausted, Wawa put a stop to their fun. At this point, she had to...

Joseph's relentless pounding battered Wawa's pussy past pleasure and straight into unsexy pain, hence the stopping of the proceedings...

"How was I ?" Joseph asked Wawa as they lay in bed, side by side, and the two of them smiled at one another.

Wawa gently kissed Joseph's hand, and nodded. The brother had performed well, but unlike a lot of women, Wawa had never been much for pillow talk.

She felt pleasurably sore, all over, but especially down below, after the rough, yet sweet loving that Joseph just laid on her.

"That was great," Wawa whispered to herself, listening to Joseph as he snored loudly next to her. Apparently sex with her had worn him out, in spite of his youthful energy and masculine prowess.

The London stud had great potential, and Wawa was definitely going to enjoy teaching, training and molding Joseph into a great lover. The brother definitely had what it took...

We are all each other's teachers one way or another, Wawa thought. She would teach Joseph, like a certain Sudanese did for her, about a decade ago, in a faraway land called Saudi Arabia.

Who knows ? If Joseph proved himself worth keeping, Wawa might persuade him to embrace her faith and then claim him.

The idea of staying in England had its appeal. Wawa thought about her life and all the places she'd been, and smiled.

She'd long ago learned to stop making big plans and enjoy the moment, even though it was always fun to fantasize...

Acknowledgements

Special thanks to my good friends Afaf Ali Alzahrani (whom I met at Carleton University in Ottawa, 2012-2014) and my good friend and former roommate Hamoud Alharbi.

As a new Muslim from a Haitian Catholic background, I love my Islamic faith even as I seek to reconcile my penchant for erotic fiction writing and expressing political thought through writing.

My friends made the Kingdom of Saudi Arabia, distant though it may be, with its beauty, wonders and pitfalls, come alive for me.

Sincerely,

Steeves Volmar-Cherenfant A.K.A. Suleiman El-Hayiti.

Ottawa, Canada. February 3, 2018.

491

www.ingramcontent.com/pod-product-compliance
Lightning Source LLC
Chambersburg PA
CBHW031141050726

47495CB00018B/247